# LAUGHING ALL THE WAY

LINDA BLESER

MIA SUMMERS

STERLING & STONE

# LAUGHING ALL THE WAY

## Chapter One

Noelle sat in front of the green screen, waiting for the "live" signal. Her assistant Gretchen held up three fingers, then two, then mouthed, "You're on."

Noelle put on her best camera-ready smile. "Hello, welcome to Your Social Media Source's weekly video. I'm Noelle Hamilton, and today we'll be discussing the movie *Over the Rainbow Bridge* by that guy who everyone thinks is a great romance writer, even though his books are depressing and there's never a happy ending. Yeah, you know the guy I'm talking about. I won't mention his name."

She held up a book with the author's name in large text across the cover and pointed. "*This* guy."

She slapped the book face down on the table. "So first off, the title. It reminds me of that poem everyone posts when their dog or kitty cat dies. Let me assure you that no animals die in this movie, which took some of the fun out of it for me."

She smiled into the camera. "Just kidding. I love animals." She paused for effect. "Other people's animals."

She continued. "So yeah, the love story. People kiss, break up, make up, then kiss some more. And just when you think it's going to be some great romance, someone dies." She rolled her eyes.

Gretchen gave her the *wrap-it-up* sign.

"You know, some people say Romeo and Juliet is a romance. It's not. It's a tragedy, and so is this movie. A romance, first and foremost, must have a happy ending. The only thing happy about this movie was that it ended. Watch it if you must, but don't say I didn't warn you."

Noelle gave her signature sign-off gesture, a two-finger sideways slicing motion followed by an upturned peace sign. "That's all for now. Noelle Hamilton, signing off."

Gretchen disconnected the camera. "That was great, really great," she gushed. "Maybe a *teeny* bit harsh?"

Noelle smiled. "That's why my subscribers come back. They want the unvarnished truth, not some Pollyanna talk."

Gretchen nodded, anxious to please as always. Her twin side buns wobbled. Noelle was accustomed to the younger woman's unwarranted hero worship, but it didn't sit right with her.

"You have to stop being such a people pleaser," Noelle told her assistant. "No one gets far in this world by trying to please everyone."

Gretchen's head jerked up and down like one of those bobble-head figures. Noelle patted her on the shoulder. There was still hope for the girl, given enough time. At least her heart was in the right place.

She did a quick video edit while Gretchen cleared the in-house studio for the next influencer. God, how she hated that word: *influencer*. It sounded amateurish to her, like someone performing simply to gain viewers. She preferred the term *content creator*. It wasn't about how many subscribers she had, but giving brutally honest reviews to the ones that kept coming back. Those were her people, and she owed them her best, most honest review, no matter how harsh.

With the clip edited, she helped Gretchen process and upload the video, surprised and pleased when Gretchen got it right on the first try. "Great job," she said.

Gretchen's eyes lit up, and her face glowed under Noelle's praise. Noelle had learned early on that positive reinforcement worked best for Gretchen in the same way you'd train an overly eager puppy. But she was a quick learner and independent thinker, which Noelle required in an assistant.

"What do you want for Christmas?" Gretchen asked.

"Huh?" Had she missed the first part of this conversation? When did the subject turn to one of her least favorite holidays? "I, umm … I hadn't given it much thought." Or any, for that matter.

Gretchen let out a long sigh. "I'm going to ask my parents for an e-bike because biking to work isn't cutting it."

Noelle blinked in disbelief. "Your parents still buy you Christmas presents?"

"Sure. Don't you, uh…?"

"No." Noelle couldn't remember the last present she got from her parents. Maybe a Barbie doll when she was six. She cleared her throat. "Don't you think you should buy your own e-bike? I mean, you're an independent young woman with a well-paying job."

Gretchen gave her those doe eyes and nodded. "Yeah. I guess you're right." But she didn't sound convinced.

"I'll let you finish up here," Noelle said. "I've got a meeting with Stuart. Hopefully, it won't take long."

She headed into the general manager's office, surprised

to see some of the others already seated. Stuart stood, towering over them all. Since he was barely five-foot-five, he always made sure to stand when everyone else was sitting. He was nearly a decade older than the rest of them, but he tried desperately to fit in. Today, he was wearing a slouchy sweatshirt, cargo pants, and neon running shoes. Noelle often wondered if he went home and immediately changed into something more age-appropriate.

"So gang," he said, rubbing his hands together. "It seems we have a problem." He gave a stern glance at everyone around the room. "The ratings are down from last quarter. Everyone will need to get their engagement numbers up fast, or we're going to start losing advertisers."

His gaze landed on Noelle. She knew that look. It was both a challenge and a threat. And it wasn't the first time he'd implied her job was in danger.

"So, to that end," he continued, "I've come up with a few assignments that I think will help you all increase your numbers." He went around the room, handing out manila envelopes.

When Noelle saw the name on the front of her envelope, she groaned inwardly. No, anything but this.

Stuart stopped in front of her. "I think this will be perfect for you."

She looked away, struggling not to argue. If this was her last chance to save her job, she'd barrel through it, no matter how much she hated the thought.

"The town is called Evergreen Creek, and their claim to fame is that they're known as *Christmas Town USA*," Stuart explained, ignoring Nicolle's silence.

Wonderful, she thought, keeping a stoic look on her face. "Is it because of my name?" she asked.

Stuart's smile was patronizing. "Well, it is a great hook, don't you think?"

Of course, when your name is Noelle, people assume you love Christmas. Not true. But Stuart didn't know that, so she didn't think this was a personal attack. *Christmas Town USA*. She took a deep breath and let it out with a sigh, then pasted an insincere smile on her face. "It'll be fun," she said.

Stuart patted her on the back. "I knew I could count on you." Then he added with a smile, "Have a holly jolly Christmas!"

Noelle got up to leave. She imagined Christmas Town USA as a tourist trap with crazed locals, a manufactured winter wonderland, and all the corny Christmas paraphernalia they could drum up. It was the last place she wanted to be. But maybe that was a good thing. She could bring her signature snark to all the phony Christmas cheer. Maybe she *was* the right person for the job.

Her lack of enthusiasm starkly contrasted with Gretchen's reaction when she told her they were going on an out-of-town assignment. She clapped her hands together and hopped up and down, barely able to contain her excitement. "Oh, it'll be wonderful," she said. "A Christmas wonderland." Her eyes sparkled, and Noelle just knew that Gretchen would show up in some sparkly Christmas sweater with dangling Christmas tree earrings.

Could this get any worse?

"Do you think there'll be reindeer?" Gretchen held her hands palms together in prayer mode.

"God willing, and the creek don't rise."

"Huh?"

Noelle chuckled. "Just something my grandfather used to say." She smiled at the memory. "Yes, I'm sure there will be reindeer, gingerbread houses, candy canes, and all that other Christmas cra…" She stopped, seeing how

Gretchen's eyes lit up like a child on Christmas morning. Her voice softened. "All that other Christmas stuff."

"I can't wait," Gretchen said.

"Neither can I." But not for the same reasons. She could already imagine the sly comments she'd make about all this Christmas hoopla. It should be a goldmine.

Noelle locked up the studio, said goodbye to Gretchen, and trudged home. Her apartment was only a few blocks from work. There was only a dusting of snow on the ground, but she made a mental note to pack a warm jacket, boots, and gloves for their trip to Christmas Freaking Town, USA.

She turned on the light in her sparse apartment, which was purposely devoid of Christmas decorations. All except the snow globe her grandfather had given her when she was twelve. But that wasn't really a Christmas decoration. It was simply a winter scene: laughing children skating on a frozen pond, their scarves billowing behind them. Pine trees dusted with snow served as a wintery backdrop.

She gave it a shake, delighted as she was years ago when the snow fell in a fluffy white blizzard. It was charming and happy, everything her childhood was not. "I miss you, Grandpa," she whispered. He'd been the rock holding it all together after her parents split. Then he died, and her life hadn't been the same since.

Noelle pushed the snow globe aside and shuffled through the mail she'd tossed on the counter. She recognized her mother's handwriting and tore open the envelope. The obligatory Christmas card was generic, probably picked up at the dollar store. It didn't even say "to my daughter," which would have been nice. Just "Happy Holidays," with her mother's signature scrawled below it.

She put it on the refrigerator next to the card from her father. One, from Portland, Oregon, and the other, from

Tampa, Florida. It wasn't enough that they got divorced — they had to move as far away from each other as possible. And her. She was equidistant from each of them in New York City and hadn't seen either in person in years. There was the occasional phone call to keep up with each other's lives and a birthday video chat where she awkwardly opened Amazon boxes shipped directly off her wish list. Happy birthday to me.

She pulled a suitcase out of her closet and started gathering sweaters, leggings, and scarves. Evergreen Creek was upstate, at the foothills of the Adirondacks. Snowfall was estimated at eighty thousand feet a week. Or thereabouts.

Boots. She'd definitely need boots. She looked around, trying to decide what else she might need. At the last minute, she tossed in a book. There was sure to be downtime between filming all the Christmas hoopla.

Once she was packed, she sat at her kitchen table and opened the folder Stuart had given her. All the details were on the info sheet. The mayor was a man named Colin Bennet. No picture. Probably some stodgy old man who'd follow her around telling her what she could and couldn't film. Well, she'd set him straight. No one told her how to do her job, not even the Mayor of Christmas Town USA.

She pulled out her phone and did a search for Evergreen Creek. Jeez, it was almost to Canada! Maybe she should add snowshoes to her packing list. The town was small, with a central town square. According to her paperwork, most of the activities would be held there. Nearby were the community center, town offices, and recreation center. These were also marked for festival events. At least she wouldn't need a car to get around. Or snowshoes, for that matter.

She added the manila envelope to her suitcase with a sigh. It was going to be a long, long week.

# Chapter Two

COLIN STEPPED through his front door, took a deep, invigorating breath, and smiled. God, he loved this town! He waved to Priscilla, his next-door neighbor, who was getting in her car to open the library. She'd been the town librarian since he was in grade school and never missed an opportunity to tell him so.

"Morning, Mayor," she called out. She could have called him Colin, or "young man," as she had when he was a boy, but always called him *Mayor* as if she took personal responsibility for getting him elected. It wasn't as if she'd handed him a book titled *How to Become the Youngest Mayor in Evergreen Creek's History.*

She glanced up at the sky. "Looks like snow."

"Let's hope so. We have a lot of activities planned for the Christmas Festival."

"Looking forward to it," she said, stepping into her car.

A young boy in a backward-facing baseball cap whizzed by on his bike. "Morning, Mayor," he called, tossing a newspaper to Colin.

Colin caught it mid-air. "Thanks, Max. How are those grades coming along?"

The boy kept going, raising one hand in the air in a backward wave, which could have meant just about anything. Colin smiled. Max was a good kid, and with a bit of extra tutoring, he'd have those grades up in no time.

Colin tucked the newspaper under his arm and stepped into his car. First stop, Evergreen Creek Coffee Cafe, for his morning caffeine fix. When he arrived, Katie had his order ready. "How's your mother doing?" he asked.

"Much better. She's home from the hospital and driving everyone crazy." She said it with the smile of someone relieved to be able to joke about it once the health scare was over.

Colin held out a ten-dollar bill, but she refused to take it. "Coffee's on us, Mayor."

He'd given up arguing about it months ago and instead stuffed the ten-dollar bill into the tip jar. That way, everyone was happy.

Colin stopped at Coach Murphy's table to congratulate him on the winning hockey game. Then, he headed for his usual table in the back, as was his weekday morning routine. Everyone in town knew they could stop by for an informal chat, especially those who were intimidated to come into the Mayor's office.

He spotted Geoff, one of the town's most talented artists, glancing his way. It was obvious Geoff wanted to chat, so Colin waved him over. Geoff's mop of blond curls bounced as he strode over.

He sat across from Colin and leaned forward, both elbows on the table. "I have some ideas for the ice carving event," he said. His voice became animated as he gestured. "I'm thinking big, avant-garde, with a passing nod to the political climate."

Colin appreciated his enthusiasm, if not his ideas. "Well, that's very interesting," he said, raising one eyebrow. "I'm sure it would be a fabulous sculpture. But, and this is just a suggestion, I think we should aim for something a bit more traditional."

Geoff nodded, setting his mop of curls bouncing. "Yeah, I hear what you're saying. More traditional, like maybe a life-size gingerbread house! Or, I don't know, I just want it to be special this year since so many people will be watching."

Colin nodded, then stopped. "So many?"

"Yeah, haven't you heard? Noelle Hamilton is coming."

Colin shook his head. He had no idea what Geoff was talking about.

At Colin's blank stare, Geoff continued. "*The* Noelle Hamilton of YouTube fame. She's coming here to do a video about our town. And she'll be covering the Christmas Festival as well." Geoff shook his head, sending his blond curls spinning. "She's got like a billion followers."

Colin's eyes widened. "That's a good thing."

"Sure is."

Colin wasn't a big social media guy, but even he knew that having that many followers was impressive. And she was coming here? All that publicity would surely help put them over the top of their fundraising goals.

"Plus, I've been dying to meet her," Geoff said, interrupting Colin's train of thought. "I wonder if she'd maybe do a show featuring some of my artwork."

Colin took out a pen. "What did you say her name was?"

"Noelle Hamilton."

Colin scribbled the name on the back of a napkin, intending to look her up later. But that wasn't necessary.

Geoff pulled out his phone, clicked a few buttons, and turned the screen to Colin.

His first thought was that she was gorgeous. Reddish brown hair he'd heard referred to as auburn. A smattering of freckles across her rose-tinted cheeks and pert little nose. Colin had always been a sucker for freckles. But it was her eyes that captivated him. They were a bright emerald green that seemed both mysterious and sincere at the same time. He could see why she had so many followers. She made a person feel as if she was talking directly to them with a smile, a secretive wink, a tilt of her head.

But then her words started to sink in. He listened for as long as he could, then gestured for Geoff to turn the video off. "Is she always this negative?"

"Negative?" He shrugged. "I guess she's a bit snarky, but that's her trademark."

"Her trademark is making fun of people?" Colin frowned. "That wasn't exactly what I had in mind for our town."

"Oh, don't worry," Geoff said, brushing off Colin's concern. "People get it. She can be snarky, but she's always honest."

"Sometimes a person can be too honest. Especially if it hurts someone else." Colin was determined to watch more of Noelle Hamilton's videos when he had time so he could decide for himself, and it had nothing at all to do with those captivating green eyes.

Colin checked his watch. He had a few more minutes before the Town Hall meeting. He finished his coffee and started back to the office. He was on his way into the meeting when Angela Cooper, the Board's treasurer, stopped him. She handed him a manila folder. "Here are the treasury reports you asked for."

Colin tucked the folder under his arm. "Thanks."

She reached up and straightened his collar, then brushed imaginary lint off his shoulders. "Gotta look like a proper mayor," she said with a maternal smile.

Colin smiled back. Angela was the closest thing to family he had. "I'll make you proud," he said.

She pinched his cheek. "You always do."

Colin couldn't help but notice the worry lines on her forehead. He made a point to talk to her about it after the meeting.

He was greeted with smiles around the conference table. He nodded to each and everyone in turn. He'd surrounded himself with good people, which wasn't hard to do in a town as close-knit as Evergreen Creek.

The Board's secretary had already passed out agendas, and Colin glanced down the list. Under *New Business,* he noted the item *Your Social Media Source.* So that's how he was going to find out about the so-called YouTube Queen's arrival.

After a quick round of "how ya been's," they started the meeting. Angela gave the treasurer's report and then turned the meeting over to Colin.

"First order of business is the new roof for Emerald Creek Elementary School. As Angela has reported, we don't have the funds in the treasury at the moment to cover it. But that's about to change. Our last fundraiser wasn't as successful as I would have liked, but I have high hopes for this year's Christmas Festival."

One of the Board's directors interrupted. "Not to mention that industry in town has dried up. All that's left is tourism."

Colin nodded. "True, but we have plans to build our industrial market and bring more jobs to the area. Until then, I'm counting on all of us to work hard to make the

Christmas festival successful. That will pay for the new roof and put us in the black for the new year."

Angela spoke up. "I have no doubt it will be more successful than last year. And the year before. Each year, we have more fundraising events, bringing in more tourists and money. It's been a success since the first Christmas Festival you created five years ago."

Colin smiled. Everyone in the room already knew the Christmas Festival had been his idea in the first place. He wasn't one to boast, but Angela didn't waste an opportunity to do it for him. She had been his mother's best friend and one of his biggest cheerleaders since he was young. She'd sat beside his mother at every soccer game, school play, and graduation ceremony he could remember. When his parents died, Angela stepped up and became the substitute mother he needed. And she was still there for him, working by his side and making sure he always had someone to lean on, talk to, and remind him of his legacy.

They'd moved on to new business, and the secretary informed Colin that they'd been contacted by *Your Source Media Company* about doing a series of videos highlighting the Christmas Festival. So that must be the company Noelle Hamilton worked for. "You make it sound like it's a done deal," he said.

The secretary stumbled over her words, "Well, we wouldn't move forward without your approval, but when they contacted us, we jumped at the opportunity."

"Of course," he said, easing her concerns. "Any publicity is good publicity, right?"

He glanced around the table. "Do we need to vote?"

Angela shook her head. "We just need you to sign off on it."

"Done," he said, turning to the secretary. "Get back to them and give them the go-ahead."

She gave a relieved nod and wrote on her copy of the agenda. Colin knew it was just a formality. They'd already put the plan into motion. But he made a mental note to have a discussion with this Noelle character. It was imperative that the Christmas Festival was a success. He wasn't about to let her turn his town into her personal laugh track.

With that last bit of business taken care of, the meeting was adjourned. Angela stopped Colin on their way out. "Why don't you come over for dinner tonight?"

"I would love to," Colin said. "But I have a meeting with the Christmas Festival Planning Committee tonight, which will probably run late. Can I have a rain check?"

She reached up and tousled his hair. "Of course. You have a permanent rain check. And would it sound too motherly for me to say you're working too hard?"

"Not at all. But you know we have a lot riding on the festival's success. I'll do everything in my power. I can relax when it's over."

"Fair enough," she said. "I'll hold you to that."

He recognized the look she gave him, which usually meant a lecture was coming. She said, "I know how much you love Christmas…"

"Just like Mom," he interrupted.

Her face softened as he knew it would. "Yes, your mother loved Christmas. But it was all about family and spending time together. Not working 24/7 to run a town event."

"This town *is* my family."

She shook her head. "I think she might have wanted more for you, like a wife and a family."

"There's time for that," Colin said. "For now, my obligation is to this town."

She reached up and cupped his cheek with a slight

shake of her head. Her silence spoke volumes, but he knew that he had her love and support no matter what.

He went into his office and noted that Kelly, his assistant, had left paperwork on his desk that needed to be signed. He took care of the paperwork, made a few phone calls, and then went over the program for the festival. Everything had to be just right.

Hours later, there was a knock at his door. He looked up, surprised to find Angela standing there with a covered dish. "I figured you'd still be working," she said. "I brought you dinner."

Colin glanced at his watch, surprised to see it was nearly eight o'clock. He straightened up and stretched his back. "Thanks. I hadn't realized how late it was."

"Of course not." She patted his arm. "Eat."

He unwrapped the dish, releasing a fragrant cloud of steam. Inside was a generous helping of pot roast and mashed potatoes covered with a dark, rich gravy. His stomach growled in anticipation, and he dove into the meal.

Angela watched him eat. When he was finished, she reached into her tote bag and pulled out a packet of home-made chocolate chip cookies.

Colin laughed. "Cookies for the cookie monster, huh?"

"Always." She took the dish and turned to go. "Try not to work too late, okay?"

"No lecture?"

"You can recite it by heart, so I'll save my breath."

Colin stood and gave her a hug. "Work too hard, blah blah blah, get some rest, blah blah, workaholic, blah…"

Angela swatted his arm. "I never say blah."

He watched her leave, a smile on his face. As much as he teased her, it was nice that someone was looking out for him. He'd make it up to her once this festival was over.

## Chapter Three

EVERGREEN CREEK WAS a short flight from New York City to upstate New York. Short in distance but miles apart in culture. Not that Noelle was a snob, but ... okay, maybe a bit of a snob. It's just that the city had everything she needed, all within walking distance. What did Evergreen Creek have? Did they even have a decent coffee shop?

From what she could see, the town looked like a Norman Rockwell version of Christmas Town USA, with gingerbread-trimmed houses and snow-capped mountains in the distance. The twinkling Christmas lights made it postcard pretty, at least from where she stood. Even the air smelled fresher, crisp, and clean.

Gretchen bounced up and down. "I can't wait to see the festival," she gushed. "Can you?"

Noelle gave a noncommittal *mmm*. "Luckily, we don't have to wait long. It starts tomorrow."

Gretchen smiled. "And lasts all week long!" She pulled out a list of events she'd downloaded from Evergreen Creek's website: *Christmas Town USA*. "A snowmobile parade! Have you ever heard of such a thing?"

"Never."

"An ice sculpting contest, a gingerbread house work-shop, Christmas carol karaoke, and a tree-lighting ceremony."

It was everything Noelle feared it would be.

Gretchen waved. "Oh. Over there." She pointed to a man holding up a sign with their names on it.

"Guess that's our ride." Noelle strode over to the man and held out her hand. "Noelle Hamilton."

The man bobbed a head full of blond curls. "I know. I'm your biggest fan. I've watched all of your videos." He finally realized he was still squeezing her hand and let go. "I'm Geoff. I'm your driver."

Gretchen was uncharacteristically silent. Noelle turned to find Gretchen staring at Geoff with impossibly wide eyes and a blush coloring her cheeks. She couldn't remember the last time Gretchen was speechless. Interesting.

Geoff grabbed their suitcases and led them from the terminal. Noelle had visions of a green pickup with a Christmas tree tied in the bed like all those country-cozy Christmas placemats, holiday cards, and Hallmark orna-ments. But no, Geoff led them outside to a cherry-red Camry. How disappointing. She'd already started writing the pickup truck story in her head. Oh well, she was sure there'd be plenty of material to work with once they got into town.

Turned out she was right. As they drove into town, Noelle took note of the Bavarian-themed Main Street. Geoff pointed out the town's giant thermometer with the coldest Christmas marked on it and the towering pine tree in the town square with a rideable train circling around it. "Oh, this is going to be great, right, Gretchen?"

"Huh?"

Noelle elbowed Gretchen, who dragged her gaze off the back of Geoff's head. "Yeah, great."

They pulled up beside the Christmas train. "A little over the top," Noelle murmured. She turned to Gretchen. "I wonder if the mayor will greet us in a Santa suit?"

She was half joking. That is until the mayor stepped off the train wearing a Santa suit, followed by a high-school band in full regalia playing Christmas tunes. Noelle was horrified to hear Gretchen singing along, "…*laughing all the way, ha ha ha!*"

It was so over the top ridiculous that Noelle couldn't help laughing as well.

The man in the Santa suit walked over. Underneath the costume, the wig, and false beard were twinkling eyes and a killer smile. "Colin Bennet," he said by way of introduction.

Noelle was impressed by his handshake. Not too firm, not too soft. "Noelle Hamilton," she said with a final shake before removing her hand from his grip.

"Your reputation precedes you."

She cocked her head. Good or bad, she wondered. Not that his opinion would have any impact on her videos. "This is Gretchen, my assistant."

Colin looked from Gretchen to Geoff, then back again. "Nice to meet you." He turned back to Noelle. "Would you like me to show you around town a bit?"

She held up her camera. "Would you mind if I took a few shots for the lead-in?"

"Be my guest." Colin led them around the town square, pointing out the giant Christmas tree, which would be lit on the last day of the festival. "Everyone in town turns up for the tree lighting," he said.

Noelle didn't miss the obvious pride in his voice. She

wished he'd take the fake beard off so she could see if his face matched his rich voice.

He led them to the square where the ice carving contest would be held.

"I'm in charge of that," Geoff piped up.

Noelle turned, surprised to see he was still with their little group. They passed the local watering hole, whose original name was covered and replaced with the name *Blitzen's*.

"So, where are the rest of the reindeer?" Noelle quipped.

Colin frowned, then turned away.

*No sense of humor*, she thought. She turned to Gretchen. "Guess they're out playing their reindeer games."

Gretchen stifled a giggle.

Colin continued walking. "This is where the Christmas marketplace will be set up, with local vendors and businesses taking part." He pointed. "Over there in the Community Hall is where we'll have the gingerbread house contest and hand out ribbons for best fruitcake."

Noelle snorted.

Colin ignored her. "For the kids, we'll have games, like pin the tail on the reindeer."

"Why not pin the red nose on the reindeer?"

He gave her the side eye. "I'll take that into consideration. Would you like to be on the games committee? We could use more ideas."

"I, umm." Noelle stammered. *Was he serious?*

Colin grinned, and Noelle saw a definite *gotcha* in his smile. Which was weird, considering he looked exactly like Santa Claus. People waved as they walked by. Children hopped up and down with excitement. Colin stayed in character with an occasional "Ho Ho Ho."

He turned to Noelle. "This town means the world to

me. Remember that when you're poking fun at us." He walked away, smiling and waving to the crowd.

Noelle was speechless. "Did you hear that?"

Gretchen bit her bottom lip.

Geoff spoke up. "Why don't I show you where you'll be staying?"

Noelle glanced at Colin's back as he walked away. "Fine with me," she said.

The Evergreen Lodge was a short walk from the town square. At first sight, it lived up to its name, with log construction and a wooden wraparound porch. Wide Adirondack chairs lined the porch, interspersed with pots of red and green poinsettia plants. A swirl of smoke drifted lazily from a weathered stone chimney.

Gretchen gazed at the lodge with her mouth open. "We're staying here?"

Geoff jumped in to assure her. "It's really nice here. My uncle is the manager, and he's given you two of his best rooms. Each one has a small kitchenette and a balcony view."

"I'm sure it will be lovely," Noelle said. She secretly hoped there was a deer head mounted on the wall. She could name it and use it as a running joke throughout the entire week. Maybe she'd call it Colin. No, that would only work if it was a donkey. She chuckled at her own joke.

Inside, they were met by Geoff's uncle Robert. "Welcome, welcome," he said. "Let me show you to your rooms."

"I'll grab their luggage from my car," Geoff said.

With that, Gretchen and Noelle were led to adjoining rooms. The four-poster beds were deep and luxurious, covered with fluffy duvets and pillows. There was a small desk and a kitchenette with a microwave, stove, and refrigerator. Noelle had no intention of cooking, but she would probably put the microwave to good use.

She walked to the balcony doors and admired the view. She could get used to this.

Geoff arrived with their luggage. Noelle scrambled for her purse to give him a tip, but Geoff held his hand up. "No, no. It was my pleasure. And if there's anything you need while you're here, please let me know." He made a slight bow. "At your service."

When he and his uncle left, Gretchen turned to Noelle. "Isn't he adorable?"

"Which one?"

Gretchen giggled. "Geoff, silly."

"Just remember, we have a job to do here."

Gretchen gave a smart salute. "Yes, boss."

# Chapter Four

THE FOLLOWING DAY, Noelle showered and dressed. It was going to be cold, so she added layers, finishing with a down vest. She pulled on a pair of socks and short boots since the forecast was predicting snow. She packed everything she needed in a tote bag, slung it over her shoulder, and knocked on Gretchen's door. "Are you ready…?" She stopped. She'd never seen Gretchen's hair down before. It was long and flowing, with sexy Jessica Rabbit waves. "Are you wearing make-up?"

"Just a touch." Gretchen blushed, turning her cheeks a deep pink. Or maybe that was make-up as well?

"Hmmm." Noelle shook her head. "Is this for that mop-headed boy, Geoff?"

Gretchen smiled. "He's way cute. And I love his curly hair."

Noelle rolled her eyes. "Need I remind you we're only here for a week?"

Gretchen shrugged one shoulder. "Doesn't mean I can't have some fun while I'm here."

Changing the subject, Noelle asked, "So where's this coffee shop Geoff recommended?"

"Right around the corner. We can walk there."

Noelle packed up her tote bag. "God knows what kind of swill they're serving at this so-called coffee shop. But at least we can get some work done while we're there."

As they walked, Gretchen admired the houses along the street. "It's really kind of cute here," she said.

Noelle's lips lifted in a half-smirk. "Maybe." Actually, now that Gretchen mentioned it, the little town did have a certain whimsical flair. The houses had gingerbread trim and scalloped shutters. Festive wreaths adorned every doorway, and brightly lit Christmas trees could be spotted behind the front windows. People who didn't even know them waved as they walked by. Noelle found that a bit weird.

They reached the Evergreen Creek Coffee Cafe. A little bell tinkled when they opened the door. Noelle looked around. The coffee house was bright and clean. Charming. A bakery case displayed blueberry scones, cinnamon rolls, pastries, and donuts. Gretchen ordered a caramel macchiato and a raspberry Danish.

"Just coffee for me," Noelle said. "Black, no sugar."

She pulled out her wallet, but the barista waved her away. "No charge. You're a celebrity! Besides, we appreciate all you're doing for our little town."

*Ouch.* Maybe they wouldn't be so amenable once she started broadcasting.

They took a seat at a round cafe table. Noelle took a sip of her coffee and sighed. It was excellent. She hadn't expected much in this little backwater town, but the coffee was rich and aromatic. She barely had her first sip when a rosy-cheeked woman stopped at the table.

"You must be Noelle Hamilton. I've heard so much about you."

"So you've seen my show?"

"Well, no. I'm not much into that Tik-Tocky stuff. Just call me old-fashioned. But I've heard wonderful things about your show."

Noelle smiled. "Thank you. I'm looking forward to covering the town's festivities."

"Be sure to stop by my booth for a special gift. A holiday mug rug."

"Mug rug?"

"Yes. It's a little quilted coaster to set your coffee mug on top of. I make them myself. You'll see. Just stop by my vendor tent. *Mug Rugs by Maxine.*"

"I'll be sure to stop by," Noelle said.

The woman — Maxine, she assumed — waved and turned to leave.

Noelle turned to Gretchen and muttered, "Mug Rug?"

Gretchen simply shook her head.

Each time Noelle tried to get some work done, more people stopped and introduced themselves, gushing about her show. Everyone was so *nice*. It was exhausting.

She pulled out her notebook to make plans for their viewing schedule. Each time they got started, someone else would stop by to say how much they were looking forward to her segment about their town. Were they just being nice to her so she'd put a positive spin on the videos? Or were they really this upbeat and happy?

Then, all the attention shifted away from her as someone walked in the door. People waved and called out, "Morning, Mayor."

"Oh, look," Gretchen said. "It's the hot mayor."

"I think he was hotter as Santa Claus."

Colin looked over, and Noelle felt her stomach roll and

tumble. When she'd first heard about this job, she imagined the mayor would be some grizzled, stodgy old man. But damn, he *was* cute without that big white beard and red hat. Not to mention all the Santa padding. He seemed to have an excellent physique under all that. Not that she was looking or anything.

Had he heard her stupid comment? He grabbed his coffee, nodded to a few people, then walked out. The room buzzed, and Noelle caught bits of puzzled conversation about how unusual it was for him to leave like that. Was it because of her?

Before she could feel bad about it, Geoff popped over and sat at their table. "That was weird," he said.

"What's that?"

"The Mayor. He usually sits at that back booth, unofficially holding business for people who stop by. Sometimes you want to talk to the Mayor but don't want to bother making an appointment, you know? So he sits here with his coffee for an hour or so, and everyone knows he's open for business, no matter how small."

"Coffee with the Mayor."

"Yeah! That's what we should call it. *Coffee with the Mayor.* I'll tell him you thought of it."

Noelle made a swiping gesture with her hand. "No need. Really."

Geoff shrugged. "Probably just had a lot to do today with the festival starting." He pulled out his phone. "Anyway, I promised Gretchen I'd show you some pictures of my art."

Noelle glanced at Gretchen, who tilted her head with an innocent smile. With a deep sigh, Noelle took the phone out of his hand. "Sure, I'd love to see them."

She flipped through the Instagram account with Gretchen looking over her shoulder.

"Wow, these are really good," Gretchen gushed.

She was right. They were. When Noelle agreed, Geoff blushed bright red.

"I wanted to do something really wild for the ice sculpture," he said. "But the Mayor said I should probably keep it more traditional."

"Really?" Noelle scrolled through his pictures. "But that's not you. Look at these drawings. Traditional is not in your wheelhouse."

Geoff's head nodded up and down. "So you think I should think outside the box?"

"I absolutely do," Noelle said. And if it annoyed the stick-up-his-ass mayor, even better.

It was an hour before they finished the paperwork, which would have been done in half that time if Gretchen hadn't been mooning over Shirley Temple.

"So Geoff," she said. "What is it you do around here? Besides, pick people up from the airport, that is."

"A little bit here and there. I'm working on my Masters."

"Oh? In art?"

He shrugged. "Actually, computer science. Art is my hobby. Oh, and I work at the reindeer farm part-time."

"Reindeer farm?" Was there actually such a thing? She turned to Gretchen. "Put that on the list of places we need to film."

"Got it, boss."

Might as well pick Geoff's brain while he was here. "What other things do you think we should see while we're here?" Noelle asked.

Geoff rubbed his chin. "Well, there's the Nutcracker Museum. The Christmas Carol Trolley. Skiing at Santa's Workshop."

"Scratch the skiing," Noelle said to Gretchen. "The last

time I went skiing, I sprained my ankle and had to walk with a crutch for weeks."

"No skiing," Gretchen said. "Got it."

"But other than that, this place is a goldmine."

Geoff, obviously missing the meaning behind her comment, bobbed his head and agreed. "We think it is. There's so much to see, not only at Christmas but year-round." He spoke to them both, but his eyes locked on Gretchen. "I'll be happy to show you around."

Gretchen had that dreamy-eyed expression again, and Noelle figured she wouldn't get much work out of her. "Why don't you two go on," she said. "I'll finish up here." She gave Gretchen a meaningful glance. "Be sure to take notes of any places we need to visit."

Gretchen gave her the thumbs up, then scampered off with Geoff. Noelle shook her head. She hoped this wasn't going to complicate things.

# Chapter Five

Colin left the coffee shop and headed for the Town Hall. There was too much to do today to sit and rub shoulders with people. People, meaning Noelle Hamilton. Yeah, he'd seen her holding court at the coffee shop in all her Grinch glory.

He didn't know why she got under his skin, but she did.

Angela greeted him at the door and walked inside with him. "So, how was your meeting with the video girl?

"It, uh … it went okay. I think I may have thrown her off a little by showing up in my Santa Claus costume."

Angela laughed. "You didn't."

Colin gave a sheepish shrug. "It seemed like a good idea at the time. How was I to know she hated Christmas?"

"Seriously?" Angela hung up her coat and waited.

"Maybe. Maybe not." He took the lid off his coffee and blew on the steamy surface. "She's snarky and kinda mean. She plays it off as joking, but it's not really funny."

Angela gave him a probing look. "All that from one little meeting?"

"Well, I took the liberty of looking up some of her

YouTube videos before she came. Utter rant fest. And yet, people follow her. Lots of people." He shook his head. "What kind of future is there on YouTube, anyway?"

Angela nodded. "Lots, I guess." She narrowed her eyes. "You've thought about her a lot."

"Had to. She's going to be representing our town."

Angela reached out and cupped his hand. "No. *We're* going to be representing our town. She's simply the voice behind the camera."

"I don't want to tell her how to do her job, but…"

Angela gave his hand a squeeze. "Then don't. Everything will be fine."

"I hope you're right."

He headed to his desk. There was a lot to do before things kicked off this afternoon. First off, he had a Hatfield and McCoy situation going on at the craft booths. Two rival neighbors had opted to share a table, but now they were complaining about it. Matty was selling crocheted Christmas gnomes, and Cynthia had a display of tulle-wrapped Christmas wreaths. Each of them insisted they needed a new spot far away from the other. Colin knew it wasn't about the booths or the crafts but something else. They'd had a falling out over a property dispute, which had come to a head over the summer. Still, they'd already rented their vendor space. Now, neither one was willing to forgive the other, and it was too late to change their spots.

Easy enough to fix. Maybe he could find someone willing to switch with one of the neighbors. He'd head out that way as soon as he saw what else needed to be handled.

Next on the list was Goodson's food truck, which supplied everything from sausage rolls to mac and cheese. They were a popular addition to the festivities, but there was a problem, and they were threatening to pull out. He'd have to handle this one personally.

He shuffled some papers on his desk. The owner of Blitzen's hadn't gotten their liquor permit for the drink booth. A few phone calls, and he could cross that off his to-do list.

His assistant popped her head in the doorway. "Anything I can do to help, Mayor?"

He took one look at her and shook his head. "You should be home with your feet up resting, Kelly."

She laughed. "I'm not the first woman to work in her third trimester. Besides, I know how important it is that everything's perfect for the festival."

She was right. But he didn't want her traipsing all over town in her condition. "Just a few little bumps," he said. "Nothing I can't take care of."

Kelly frowned. "Are you sure there isn't anything I can do to take some of the load off your hands?"

"Tell you what." He handed her a packet of papers. "If you can handle these phone calls, I'll go into town and handle some of the other emergencies."

She took the papers and headed for her desk, then gave him a bright smile. "Everything will be fine. Don't worry."

He shook his head. "You're the second person to tell me that. I just wish I had your confidence." Colin put on his hat and coat. "Wish me luck," he called out. Both Kelly and Angela yelled, "Luck!" as he headed out the door.

First stop: Blitzen's for an update. William met him at the door. "Good news," Colin said. "The paperwork for your liquor permit has been approved. You can pick it up in an hour."

William swiped his forehead. "Thank you! I've been running around with them all week trying to get that permit. Good to know we can open for business tonight." He held out a hand. "Thanks, mate. Drinks are on the house."

Colin gave a grateful nod. If things didn't work out, he'd need one.

He checked his phone when a text notification beeped. It was Kelly.

*Good News: Got the food truck situation taken care of. It was a misunderstanding.*

*Bad News: It's going to cost an extra thousand dollars to rent the truck for three days.*

Colin groaned. He had some wiggle room in the budget, so this wouldn't break the bank, but that new school roof would eat up most of the fundraising. He texted Kelly back.

*Good job. Thanks for taking care of that. I'll be back in the office in an hour or so.*

He went to the marketplace, where vendors were already setting up their tables. He'd tried to keep vendor rental space to a minimum to make it affordable for everyone. There were still a few empty spots, however. It was a balancing act, making the vendor tables affordable for crafters and adding to the profit column.

Seeing the creative way the vendor tables were decorated made him smile. Everyone had put a lot of work into their tables, with Christmas colors and greenery adorning every available surface. He wondered if knowing they'd be videotaped for YouTube made everyone go the extra mile. He passed tables selling homemade preserves, pottery, freshly baked nut breads, and every craft imaginable.

Familiar faces waved and smiled. That was until he got to the cantankerous neighbors. Matty was the first to jump in his face. "I paid for my booth before she did, so I should have the first choice of spots."

"Vendor spots were arranged on a random basis," Colin said. "I can put one of you in an open spot on the back row if you can't share."

"She should go," Matty said. "This is the spot I had last year. That's *my* spot."

Cynthia piped up. "He thinks this spot gets more traffic than the back row. That's why he said I should move." She shot a venomous glance at Matty. "I'm not moving. You can take your little gnomes and shove them—"

"Okay, that's enough," Colin interrupted. He looked from one to the other, then pulled out his vendor seating chart. "So let's see," he said. "Obviously, you can't both have the same spot, especially since…" He glanced over at Matty's gnomes and shook his head.

"What? What's wrong with my gnomes?"

"Yeah, what's wrong with his gnomes?" Cynthia said. "He's been working on them all year." She shrugged one shoulder. "I think they're kind of cute."

"Thanks," Matty said. "And so are your wreaths. Charlotte told me to make sure I bought one before they were all gone."

Cynthia smiled. "You just tell me which one you think she'll like, and I'll set it aside."

Colin straightened out the seating chart. "So, which one of you wants to move? I have a few extra spaces toward the back."

They both looked at him like he was crazy, "No way. We're staying here where there's more traffic."

"You sure?"

"We are," they said in unison.

Matty turned to Cynthia and muttered. "Move to the back? What is he thinking?" They both chuckled.

"I appreciate your cooperation," Colin said. "I hope you have a ton of sales." With that, Colin turned to leave. Nothing brought people closer than having a common enemy, even if he'd only played the part for a second.

He headed back to his office, hoping that was the last emergency issue he'd have to deal with before opening ceremonies.

His hopes were dashed the minute he walked in the door. Kelly stopped him before he got to his desk. "Bad news," she said. "A pipe burst in the library basement."

"Oh no. Was anything lost?"

"No, they have it under control, but we'll need to tap into the festival funds to cover repairs."

Colin's shoulders slumped.

Angela was beside him, one comforting arm around his shoulder. "It's okay. Don't let the stress get to you."

"Seems like I put out one fire, and two more pop up." He didn't have to tell her he felt like an imposter. He'd inherited this job from the best mayor that Evergreen Creek had ever had — his mother. He cast a glance at Angela. "What would Mom do?"

"Whatever she could," Angela said. "Putting out one fire at a time." She gave him a motherly squeeze. "But whatever happened, she'd never forget what's important about Christmas. It's about family and friends and spending time together. No one will remember a little gaffe or two at the festival. What they'll remember are the memories they've made."

Angela was right. His best memories were holidays

spent with his family and friends, including Angela. She was always there.

"Thank you," he said, but the words held more meaning than she'd ever know. How do you thank someone who stepped in when she was needed, who promised your mother she'd make sure you were taken care of and kept that promise? How do you thank someone who was your biggest cheerleader and always had your back?

He didn't know the answer to those questions, but he was determined to ensure that Angela always knew how grateful he was.

# Chapter Six

At noon, Noelle and Gretchen went to the high school football field for the opening ceremonies.

Gretchen turned the camera on Noelle. "This is Noelle Hamilton, coming to you from Evergreen Creek, otherwise known as *Christmas Town USA*. Yes, that's right, an entire town dedicated to Christmas. We'll be covering their week-long Christmas festival." She rolled her eyes for the camera. "An *entire* week of Christmas festivities. Can you stand it?"

They took a seat on the bleachers and watched Colin make his way to center field. He tapped his microphone. "Is this thing on? Can you hear me?"

As the crowd cheered, Colin smiled. "Welcome to our fifth annual Christmas Festival. We have five days of activities to keep you entertained, ending with the Christmas tree lighting on Christmas Eve and a visit from Santa Claus for all the children." He looked around at the audience. "And those of you still young at heart."

The children in the audience cheered. "San-ta CLAUS! San-ta CLAUS! San-ta CLAUS!"

Colin let that go on for a few minutes while the adults smiled at the excited children. He held up a hand, and the chanting dwindled down. "Santa will be here later this week. But today, we have a full day of activities."

He checked the program in his hand, identical to the ones Noelle and Gretchen held, along with everyone else.

"We're starting off with the popular marketplace, where your neighbors will be showcasing their handmade arts and crafts. I've had a look, and there are some fabulous crafts, so you might want to get there early before they're gone."

He made an *I'll tell you a secret* gesture and pretended to whisper into the microphone. "Mrs. Claus has made her popular fruitcakes, which I've heard have been soaking in brandy for two weeks. Eat it at your own discretion."

The crowd roared. Noelle turned to Gretchen. "I hate fruitcake."

"I thought everyone did."

Noelle gestured to the crowd. "Apparently not. Either that or Mrs. Claus makes some kind of magical fruitcake."

"Maybe some of them have already been into the brandy."

Noelle chuckled, intending to use that line in the video.

"At two o'clock is our yearly event, the decorated snowmobile parade. And I'm hoping we can convince our guest videographer, Noelle Hamilton, to be one of the judges." He looked directly at her, and she had a moment to wonder how he knew where she was sitting. Had he been watching for her? "How does that sound, Noelle?"

"Like my worst nightmare," she murmured. Except everyone was staring at her and cheering. This was the cheeriest crowd she'd ever seen. She held up her hand, thumbs up, and the cheers intensified. She'd make Colin pay for this later.

Gretchen clapped her hands. "This'll be fun."

Noelle scowled. Gretchen's hands stilled, then dropped to her side.

"At four o'clock," Colin continued, "we'll have the cherry pie-eating contest. Last year's champion, Bubba Brown, is challenging everyone to beat his record."

Someone in the stands stood up and leaned forward, making a muscleman gesture that did little to hide his bulging belly. "Must be Bubba," Noelle said. "Looks like he knows his way around a cherry pie."

"He's probably eaten his share of boozy fruitcakes, too," Gretchen replied.

"At five o'clock," Colin continued, "we'll serve cookies and hot chocolate in the Community Hall." He waited for the applause to die down, then pulled out a gong from a bag at his feet. He hit the gong with a resounding clang and shouted into the microphone, "Welcome to the Fifth Annual Christmas Festival! Let the festivities begin!"

People broke off into groups. Some headed for the marketplace, others in the opposite direction. Noelle assumed those people were either participants preparing for the snowmobile parade, *God help me*, or volunteers setting up some of the other events. She knew there were rooms set up with coloring pages for the children as well as a game room. It seemed as if everyone had a job to do.

Including her. She turned to Gretchen. "Ready to check out the Christmas market?"

Noelle folded the program and put it in her bag. Knowing what time activities started would help her plan her recording schedule. That was pretty sneaky of Colin, putting her on the spot to judge the snowmobile parade. But now that she thought about it, it would give her a perfect platform for her video clip.

While they walked, Noelle went over her plan for the

video. "We'll start with a general overview of all the vendors with their customers. Then we'll chat with some vendors, but I want to leave some space for voice-overs when we edit."

Gretchen nodded. "Do you want me to warn, umm, I mean clear a path for you?"

"No, I think, in this case, I'd like to take a more candid approach."

She pulled up the video recorder and started filming, speaking into the recorder. "Welcome to the Christmas Marketplace, otherwise known as Tchotchke Alley," she said dryly. She scanned the rows of booths, from home-made baked goods to handmade crafts. There were ceramic Christmas trees with tiny light bulbs, Christmas quilts, wreaths adorned with pinecones and berries, fruit-cakes, and Christmas stockings. Noelle was surprised at the quality and variety of the items as she passed by. It surprised her how many times she made a mental note to go back and take a second look at one or two items.

After a quick pass through the entire marketplace, Noelle chose a few vendor stalls that looked promising for some one-on-one. The first stop was Mrs. Claus's fruitcake, where they were urged to eat bite-sized samples from tiny plastic containers.

Gretchen dove right into it and asked for a second.

"I don't eat fruitcake," Noelle said, holding up her hand in a warding-off gesture.

"Oh, you haven't eaten fruitcake until you've tried mine," Mrs. Claus said. Noelle had tried to get her to reveal her real name, but she insisted on being called simply Mrs. Claus. She held out a sample, urging Noelle to try it. "You don't want to go on Santa's naughty list now, do you?"

"Oh, that's the last thing I want," Noelle quipped with

a knowing look into the camera. She picked the sample out of the container and took a nibble. Then another. The bourbon hit the back of her throat, offsetting the sweet cake and tangy fruit. "Oh my God," she said around a mouthful of fruitcake.

Gretchen dug for her purse. "I'll take two loaves," she said, handing Mrs. Claus a twenty-dollar bill.

Mrs. Claus put two loaves into a bag and handed Gretchen the change. "Thank you, love. Now remember, don't eat too much fruitcake and drive. It packs a punch."

Noelle believed it. That one bite gave her a tiny buzz. She could imagine what it would be like to eat a slice or two. They moved on, leaving Mrs. Claus to push her boozy fruitcake on unsuspecting customers. Or maybe they weren't so unsuspecting since some seemed to be repeat customers.

"And there you have it," Noelle said, looking directly into the camera. "Boozy fruitcakes. You can get sugared up and knocked flat on your butt at the same time." Lame, but it was the best she could do with what she had.

As they walked to the next vendor, Noelle turned to Gretchen. "That seemed kind of pricey for a fruitcake."

Gretchen reached into the bag and broke off a piece. She offered it to Noelle, who shook her head, then popped it in her mouth and moaned in ecstasy. "Worth every penny."

"Speaking of pennies, it seems like all the prices are a little inflated."

Gretchen shrugged. At the next stand, she picked up a little crocheted Christmas gnome. "Oh, isn't this adorable! I'm buying one for my mother. She collects gnomes."

Noelle rolled her eyes and held the microphone out to the booth attendant. "You are?"

"Matty Coughlin," he said, smiling for the camera. He

held up a gnome. "These are my Christmas gnomes, but I make them for other holidays as well. It's my own pattern."

"I see. And how long have you been crocheting?"

"Oh, let's see. I started when I was a fireman for the volunteer fire department. We had a lot of downtime, and my wife showed me how to crochet. It filled the time and kept my mind occupied. At first, I just made potholders and coasters, but then I heard about amigurumi. Know what that is?"

"Haven't a clue."

"I didn't either. But it's a Japanese word meaning to knit or crochet stuffed dolls or animals. Let me show you."

He bent down and lifted a bin out from under the table. It was full of tiny stuffed animals no bigger than the palm of her hand. There were teddy bears, lambs, owls, bunnies, and even a tiny hedgehog. Hard as she tried, she couldn't come up with anything snarky to say about a firefighter who crocheted adorable little animals and Christmas gnomes.

"Oh, look," Gretchen said. "This looks exactly like your cat, Damian."

Noelle took the stuffed animal and smiled. It looked exactly like her demon of a cat; it even had that haughty sneer he wore when he was up to mischief. "I'll take this one," she said. She handed him her credit card and put the stuffed cat in her pocket. "Can I ask you a question?"

"Of course."

"The prices here seem a little high. Is that normal?"

"No, it's for the fundraiser. Didn't you see the candy cane?"

"Candy cane?"

"Yeah, over by the Christmas tree in the Town Square. Geoff made one of those fundraising thermometers but in the shape of a candy cane. We're trying to raise enough money for a new roof for the school."

"Oh. A new roof."

"Yeah." He gestured to include all the vendors. "We have free table space, and we've all pledged to donate half of our profits for the school roof."

"Everyone?"

Matty nodded. "This way, we can have some fun, make a little money from our crafts, and do something good for our town."

"I, uh … I didn't know." Noelle looked around and caught Colin watching from a few booths away. Was he following her?

Gretchen picked out three more stuffed animals and paid for them, looking slightly abashed. "It's for a good cause," she explained before Noelle could comment.

They worked their way down the row of vendors, getting the same story from each one. From what Noelle was told, each vendor was given the opportunity to rent a table for a small fee and keep their profits or get the space for free and donate half their earnings to the fundraiser. Everyone jumped at the chance to participate in the fundraiser. The sense of community was overwhelming.

Each time she thought she'd found the perfect item to make fun of, she'd hear a story that had her second-guessing her intentions. Like the woman who made knitted Christmas stockings that were more decorative than functional. In her spare time, she knitted baby caps for preemies at the neonatal unit. Yeah, no comedic material there.

The woman who made crude gingerbread houses also donated a portion of her proceeds to the Children's Cancer Foundation because she recently lost her granddaughter to cancer. It was hard to make jokes about life-altering events without looking like a jerk. And that wasn't her brand. Maybe she'd have better luck with the snowmobile parade.

Just then, Colin stepped up beside her. "I hope you're enjoying our marketplace."

Noelle nodded. "I've bought a few things myself."

Gretchen held up an overflowing market bag she'd purchased. It had a giant Christmas Tree on the front. "I bought a few things, too."

Colin laughed. "I see that. We appreciate your support."

Noelle cleared her throat. "I didn't realize this was a fundraiser for the school. It seems like everyone is chipping in to do their part."

"That's the way Evergreen Creek is. We're a small but close-knit town. Everyone helps each other and looks out for their neighbor."

Noelle thought those towns only existed in sitcoms and Hallmark movies. It was surprising to actually see it in person. "Like I said, I didn't realize the festival was a fundraiser for a good cause. I'd like to take a video of the fundraising poster and update our viewers as the days progress."

"Well, you might have to wait a few hours."

"A few hours? Why's that?" Hadn't someone said the fundraising candy cane was up already?

"Geoff is making a new one," Colin said. "We had a flood in the library basement this morning, so we're hoping to make enough to cover that as well."

"Oh no! Were any books destroyed?"

Colin shook his head. "Luckily, no books were destroyed. The flooding was in the basement, so the books were safe."

"Thank goodness!"

"I gather you like books, huh?"

She nodded. "Reading is my escape. It's got me through a lot of tough times."

Colin gave her a quizzical look but didn't ask her to elaborate on what tough times she may have had. "What was your favorite book as a child?"

"*Goodnight Moon.* No, *Where the Wild Things Are.* Oh, wait, anything by Niles Nash. Gosh, I can't pick a favorite."

"I loved Niles Nash growing up, too," Colin said with a smile of recollection. "I can still recite some of his poems."

"Oh, what's your favorite?"

He gave her a searching look. "Masks." Then proceeded to recite it from memory.

*THROUGH JOURNEYS LONG, adventures far*
   *Beneath the sun and moon and stars*
   *They searched for azure all their lives*
   *And found it in the bluest skies*

NOELLE FELT a jolt in her stomach. Something about the way he recited those lines resonated in her. Was she wearing a mask? Is that why she hadn't found her soulmate? Did she even believe in soulmates?

She looked away. "I think we're done with the marketplace footage."

She turned to leave, but just then, shouting broke out. They all turned at the raised voices. "Excuse me," Colin said. He took off in the direction of the argument. Noelle followed, motioning for Gretchen to start filming.

It was a booth Noelle had stopped at earlier. Two brothers shared a table. She checked her notes. Randy and

Otis Vonn. Randy made reindeer from branches, and Otis made hot cocoa mixes in mason jars. Gretchen had bought a jar of the hot cocoa mix.

"Hey guys," Colin said. "What's the problem here?"

"He's taking up more than half the table with those reindeer sticks, for God's sake."

"How many freaking jars of cocoa do you need out?" Randy argued, his voice rising. "You can keep most of them under the table and leave a few out for people to see. They're all the same. They're *exactly* the same!"

"Doesn't matter. When I said I'd share a space with you, I assumed we'd each have half the table."

Their voices grew louder, and people were gathering to watch. Colin noticed that Gretchen was filming. He turned away from the cousins and asked her not to film this altercation.

"Why not? I said I'd cover the entire event, not just the nice parts. Do you want an honest representation or some sugar-coated fantasy?"

Colin gave a huff of annoyance. Fine, let him be annoyed. Noelle was grateful to see Gretchen was still filming as the argument escalated. Push led to a shove, then a shove led to a punch, and before she knew it, Colin had stepped between them, trying to break up the fight. Instead of breaking it up, however, he became a part of it. There was the sound of glass breaking, and antlers flew everywhere. Then they grappled on the ground, with Colin caught in the middle.

As quickly as it started, it was over. The three men stood and brushed themselves off. "Sorry, Mayor," Otis said with a sheepish grin.

Colin glared at the men. "If this keeps up, I'm going to have to remove you both. Got it?"

"Yeah," they said in unison. "Got it."

Up until now, she'd only seen the softer side of Colin. Seeing him stand up and confront the dueling brothers was kind of hot. That was until he turned on her.

"I don't want that footage shown. That's not what our town is about. This was an isolated incident."

"I don't believe you have control over *my* show."

Colin stalked away. Noelle turned to Gretchen. "How much of that did you get?"

"All of it." She frowned. "But maybe we shouldn't…"

"I'll decide," Noelle said. But when she turned and watched Colin storming away, she felt a tinge of regret. She checked her watch. "We have another hour before the next event. Let's go back to the room and drop these things off."

Back at the lodge, Noelle put her bags down and her feet up. She retrieved the toy cat she'd picked up at the marketplace. She named him Damian Two and set him on the bedside table. She liked to joke that Damian was a demon disguised as a cat, but in reality, he was a little love muffin. He followed Noelle wherever she went and was always in the mood for snuggling on her lap. When she was at the computer, he would lie across the keyboard as if to tell her she wasn't allowed to pay attention to anything but him.

Damian wasn't just a cat. He was the only living thing she loved unconditionally. He would go outside to explore, but he always came back. Having lived her life under a cloud of abandonment, that meant more to her than any false words or empty promises.

She'd never left Damian alone for this long. He was staying with Berta, a sweet elderly neighbor who adored him. Noelle often picked up grocery items for Berta at the market, so she'd jumped at the chance to repay the favor.

Noelle picked up her phone and called Berta.

She answered on the first ring. "How are you, dear?"

"I'm good. I was just calling to check on Damian." She couldn't believe she was checking on a cat like some helicopter mom.

"He's just fine. Snoozing on the couch right now. He was a little devil earlier today, however."

Noelle smiled. "How so?"

"Well, he got into my knitting basket and chased a ball of yarn all around the living room. Here, let me send you a picture."

Seconds went by. Finally, Berta came back. "How do you send a picture again?"

Noelle walked her through it, then laughed when she saw the picture. Yarn wound around chairs, through coffee table legs, over the couch, and under again.

"I could have stopped him before he made such a mess," Berta said with a laugh. "But he was having so much fun chasing that ball of yarn that I couldn't bear to take it away."

"He's living up to his name, isn't he?"

"I guess so if his name was Lovebug." She chuckled. "So what's it like where you are?"

"Hmm. Have you ever watched one of those Hallmark Christmas shows?"

"All the time."

"Well, it's like every one of them. Christmas everywhere, all the time."

"Oh, sounds delightful. I'll be sure to watch your videos." She stopped, and Noelle could almost see the frown on her face. "That is, if I can remember how to do it."

"No worries," Noelle said. "I'll text the instructions for you."

"You're a dear."

"Don't tell anyone," Noelle said. "It'll ruin my reputation."

After getting off the phone, Noelle tapped on the adjoining room door. Gretchen had changed into a red sweater with jingling bells sewn on the front. Noelle gave her a probing look.

"When in Rome," Gretchen said with a giggle.

"Remind me never to go to Rome," Noelle quipped.

Gretchen laughed. She never took offense at Noelle's smart-ass remarks. That was one of the things Noelle admired about her. Other assistants had gone running, sometimes in tears, over the least little comment. Jeez, it was as if they'd never even heard the rhyme, "Sticks and stones may break my bones, but words will never hurt me."

Chapter Seven

COLIN GREETED Noelle when she returned to the festival grounds. It was almost as if he'd been waiting for her. He glanced at his watch. "Just in time. I'll take you to the judge's stands. The snowmobiles are lining up for the parade. You'll have a chance to check each one out individually before the parade starts."

"Yeah, about that," she drawled. "Thanks for volunteering me to judge the parade."

He gave her a side glance without turning his head. "It was either that or the pie-eating contest, and you don't seem like someone who enjoys sweets."

Noelle blinked. Had he just insulted her?

"Look, I—"

He interrupted, "We appreciate you stepping up. We've never had a celebrity judge before."

Stepping up? More like thrown to the wolves. But it could work out for the best. The marketplace hadn't given her much to work with, but she had high hopes for decorated snowmobiles. That was until she arrived at the staging area.

Each snowmobile was more intricate than the last, from floating snow globes to rolling gingerbread houses. Some were bedecked with fake snow, others were covered in evergreen boughs and jingling bells. Some pulled mini floats behind them. There was a Grinch float, complete with a Grinch, and Santa's workshop with elves. Not only was there nothing to ridicule, she wasn't even sure how to judge a winner from the group. They were all outstanding.

"Do these people design stage props in their spare time?" she asked.

Colin smiled. "They take their snowmobile decorating seriously. Some of these people will start planning next year's entry as soon as the winners are announced."

Connor handed her a judging sheet. Scoring was based on creativity, visual appeal, originality, and overall appearance, scored from one to ten. This was more serious than she expected. She took her place on the judging stand and left the filming to Gretchen. She'd add her voice-over later.

She barely noticed when Colin took a seat beside her. Each entry was more impressive than the next. They were beautiful when they were parked in the staging area, but now that they were moving, it was a sight to behold. There was smoke coming out of chimneys, artificial snow inside a giant snow globe, and children in reindeer costumes scampering in front of Santa's sleigh.

"No sarcastic comment?" Colin murmured.

What was up with his attitude? "I'll save the comments for later."

"Here, I thought your comments were spontaneous, not rehearsed."

There was something about the tone of his voice that put her on edge. "And why would that make any difference?"

He turned and held her gaze. "It's a question of intent."

Her back stiffened, but she wasn't about to let his disapproval get to her. "My intent is to entertain, to say what my viewers are thinking."

"And if it hurts someone else?"

She didn't have an answer for that. If she worried about whether her comments hurt someone, it would stifle her creativity. It wasn't enough just to be snarky. It only worked if you were quick. The element of shock and surprise was what took sarcasm to the next level. She shouldn't have to explain her process to him or anyone else. The fact that she had over a million viewers spoke volumes.

Ignoring Colin's glare, she concentrated on her score sheet. Choosing a winner would be harder than she thought. Luckily, the other judge's scores would also be considered. When the parade was over, she handed her completed score sheet to Colin and got to her feet.

"Will I see you at the pie-eating contest?" His smile didn't reach his eyes.

"I'm not really much for sweets," she replied, throwing his own words back at him. She turned and stalked away.

Gretchen had come over to them and had watched at a distance. "What was that about?" she asked.

Noelle shook her head. "He's pretentious, opinionated and, and…" She stamped her foot. "Condescending."

"Yeah, but he's hot."

"Only if you like that kind of buttoned-up, self-absorbed butthead."

"Butthead? Is that the best you can come up with?" Gretchen grinned. "He must really get under your skin."

Noelle chose not to dignify that with an answer.

As it turned out, the pie-eating contest was a bit of an

upset. Bubba Brown seemed to be running away with it but inevitably started slowing down and rubbing his stomach, burping to make room for more pie. Out of nowhere came all one hundred pounds of Nellie Bloom eating pie like a contestant on *Survivor*.

The crowd started chanting, "Go Nellie, Go Nellie!"

Bubba started turning green but made a valiant attempt to catch up. Then, with a resounding smack, Nellie hit the table. "Done!"

The judges swarmed to her station. After a brief consultation, they lifted her arm in the air. "The winner is Nellie Bloom!"

Bubba turned and vomited behind the stage.

"This is gold," Noelle said to Gretchen, who was looking a little green herself. "Let's go interview the winner."

They made their way to the stage where Nellie was accepting her pie-eating medallion. She fingered the medal and smiled.

"So tell me." Noelle pushed the microphone into Nellie's face. "How did you prepare for the contest?"

"I stretched my stomach, eating a little more pie each day until I was sure I could beat Bubba. He's gotten a little too cocky. Someone had to bring him down a notch." She said it with a smile on her face. Noelle couldn't have liked her more.

"You made him barf."

"Extra credit."

Noelle laughed. This was a woman after her own heart. She wrapped up the interview and turned to leave.

"Aren't you staying for cookies and hot chocolate?" Gretchen asked.

"Do I look twelve?" She gave Gretchen a light hug.

"You go enjoy yourself. I'm going to get a head start on today's videos."

Gretchen waved and scampered away, no doubt to find Geoff. Noelle spotted Colin looking her way and decided to make a quick escape before he could tell her how she should be doing her job.

Back in her room, she was surprised at how much footage she had to work with. But a lot of it was too saccharine-sweet. She'd use it, but she needed something with the wow factor. She kept coming back to the tussle at the marketplace. Colin had asked her not to use it, but she hadn't committed one way or the other.

She decided to add a voice-over to the video. "Who knew crafting was a contact sport?" she said. "When reindeer antlers and hot chocolate mason jars vie for table space, crafts fly, and someone always gets caught in the middle. That someone was the esteemed Mayor of Evergreen Creek." She switched to footage of Colin on the ground. She felt a tiny twinge of regret but stuffed it down. Her audience expected more than sugarcoating. They wanted to see the real nitty gritty.

When Gretchen knocked on the door, Noelle was surprised to see how much time had passed. She opened the door. Gretchen held up a bag. "I brought you some coffee and Christmas cookies," she said. "They're decorated."

"Of course they are." Noelle took the bag. "Thank you." She realized she hadn't eaten in hours. Guess the cookies would have to do.

"Oh, by the way," Gretchen said, "Colin asked me to tell you he's arranged for you to visit the reindeer farm tomorrow at ten."

"Seriously?"

"That's what he said."

"Didn't Geoff say he worked part-time at a reindeer farm? I thought he was pulling my leg."

Gretchen nodded and blushed at the sound of Geoff's name. Poor girl was smitten.

Noelle groaned. "Well, at least I'll get some footage of actual reindeer. Are you coming?"

"Nope. I need to talk to a few sponsors and do some admin work. I'll catch up with you later."

"If I'm not mauled by a reindeer."

Gretchen laughed and turned to leave. "Be careful," she called over her shoulder. "Grandma got run over by a reindeer."

"Well, that's encouraging. Thanks for the cookies," Noelle called after her, then locked up and went back to work, fueled by sugar and coffee.

She put in a few more hours of editing, then sat down to read for a bit. Eventually, she grew tired of the newest domestic thriller and turned on the television. She flipped through the channels, but nothing grabbed her attention. She knew she wouldn't be able to sleep with all the caffeine running through her system, and it was still early. Since Gretchen hadn't returned, she decided to go to Blitzen's solo. Maybe a hot toddy would help her sleep.

The streets were well-lit, with festive snowflake decorations hanging from every streetlamp. She took her time, enjoying the peaceful evening. Occasionally, she'd pass someone who smiled and waved. She wasn't sure if they recognized her or were simply friendly to everyone.

When she entered Blitzen's, she was not surprised to see Gretchen and Geoff shooting darts. "Hey, kids," she said. "Anyone lose an eye yet?"

Geoff grinned. "No, but there's still time."

Noelle took a seat at the bar. "Whiskey with a shot of melatonin," she said.

The bartender gave her a blank stare, obviously missing her humor.

"How about a hot toddy?"

He gave a relieved smile. "That I can do."

She sat back and watched Gretchen and Geoff's half-hearted competition. They weren't even trying to win.

When her drink came, she let the warm combination of whiskey, honey, and lemon take the chill off. Just as she was starting to feel loose and relaxed, she heard a familiar voice. "Having a little holiday cheer?" Colin asked, coming up behind her.

She held up her drink, admiring the amber glow. "If that's what you call it."

"Nah. I wouldn't use the words *holiday* and *cheer* to describe you."

"Oh? What words would you use?" She waited a heartbeat, imagining all the negative words he could think up to describe her.

He surprised her instead. "Driven," he said. "And vulnerable."

She started to say something, but the words escaped her.

He turned to the bartender. "I'll have what she's having," he said.

She smiled. "That's one of my favorite movies."

"Yeah?" he leaned against the bar, facing her. "*When Harry Met Sally?*"

She nodded.

"Mine too," he said. "Did you know that it was Rob Reiner's mother who said that famous line?"

Noelle gave him a calculated stare. "I wouldn't have pegged you for a rom-com fan."

"I could say the same about you."

"Yeah, well, don't tell anyone. It'll ruin my reputation."

He gave a hearty laugh. "I think your reputation as an all-around Grinch is cast in stone."

"Just like my heart," she said, sipping her drink.

His gaze softened. "No. I don't think you have a heart of stone. I think you've built a stone wall around your heart to protect it. There's a difference."

She looked away. Who was this guy? One drink and he turned into an amateur psychologist.

"Want to shoot some pool?" he asked.

Grateful for the change of subject, Noelle agreed. Little did he know she'd cut her teeth playing billiards on her grandfather's pool table in his basement. She watched him walk toward the pool table, admiring the view, followed him over, and chalked her stick while he racked the balls.

"I'll let you break," he said.

"How kind of you." She took her shot, hitting the balls cleanly and sending them in every direction. Nothing fancy. She was just getting warmed up.

Colin made a nice bank shot, putting a striped ball in the pocket. That left her with solids.

She called the two in the side pocket and added a little English. It bounced off the four-ball and sunk the two in the side pocket with a satisfying *thunk*.

"Nice shot," he said.

She grinned. "Beginner's luck."

He raised an eyebrow, then watched as she proceeded to run the table, finally sinking the eight ball for a win.

"Beginner's luck, huh?"

Noelle gave a satisfied smile. "I may have played a few games before."

He racked the balls for another game. "At least you didn't hustle me out of my paycheck."

"I was tempted, but I heard your job doesn't pay much."

He chuckled. "You can say that again."

They played a few more games, finally giving up the table to another couple waiting in the wings.

Noelle finished her drink and then slipped her coat on. "I think I'll be able to sleep now."

"Because you proved your prowess as a pool shark?"

"Nope, because this hot toddy did the trick."

Colin put his own coat on. "Let me walk you back to the lodge."

"I can find my own way."

"I know, I know. You're an independent woman who doesn't need some man to take care of her. But can you please just let me recover some of my manly pride since you bruised my ego so badly at the pool table?"

"Well," she said. "Since you put it that way, okay."

As they walked past Gretchen, she said, "See you tomorrow."

"Right," Noelle said with a smirk.

## Chapter Eight

THE NEXT MORNING, Noelle stared at the clothes she'd packed. What was the appropriate dress for a reindeer farm? Boots, for sure. There were probably reindeer droppings all over the place. She chose jeans and a sweater, then layered on a down vest. She added gloves and a scarf to her tote bag just in case it got colder than it already was.

On her way out, Robert, the lodge manager, stopped her. "I just wanted to thank you," he said. "My bookings are way up, and I'm sure it's because of your videos."

"Oh, you're very welcome. You have a lovely place here."

It was true. The lobby was oak and stone, with conversation nooks surrounding a roaring fireplace. Even the Christmas stockings hung on the mantel didn't annoy her as much as it should have. There was something both charming and quaint about the lodge, and she was enjoying her stay.

Robert smiled. "If things keep up like this, we'll be fully booked by the end of the day."

Noelle couldn't help but feel a sense of pride. If her

videos were bringing more people to the lodge, that meant more people were attending the festival. The more people who attended the festival, the more money they'd raise. Now that she knew about the fundraising efforts to put a new roof on the school and repair the broken pipe in the library, she was invested in helping them meet their goals.

She stepped outside to wait for her ride to the reindeer farm. Her hopes for a horse-drawn carriage were dashed when her driver showed up on a snowmobile. She eyed the machine cautiously. Was she supposed to get on that?

The driver turned off the engine and climbed off the snowmobile. He took off his helmet, and Noelle rolled her eyes. "Colin?"

"At your service." He handed her an extra helmet and gestured for her to climb aboard.

"Seriously? Is this even safe?"

"Safe as can be. Snowmobiles are our main source of transportation in the winter, especially for places that are a little more out of the way."

"Like the reindeer farm."

"Exactly."

It wasn't Noelle's first choice of transportation, but she wouldn't let Colin see that. She took the helmet he gave her, fastened the strap under her chin, and then climbed on the back of the snowmobile. Colin grinned, then put on his own helmet and sat in front. He reached behind and grabbed her hands, wrapping them around his waist, then started the engine. With a roar, they took off, and Noelle's grip on his waist tightened. She closed her eyes and tried not to think about all the things that could go wrong.

On the bright side, she didn't have to talk to Colin over the roar of the snowmobile. At least not until the snowmobile broke down with a metallic sputter. Colin tried starting it up again, but all it did was whine, which is what Noelle felt like doing. Why had she let him talk her into getting on this beast?

Finally, Colin gave up. He took off his helmet and radioed for help, then turned to Noelle. "It'll be a little while before anyone arrives."

Noelle took off her helmet and reached for her phone. "I'll just have Gretchen send an Uber."

Colin laughed. "Good luck finding an Uber driver in Evergreen Creek. Besides, look around. We're in the middle of a field. You'd have better luck calling a helicopter."

"Do you have helicopters in Evergreen Creek?"

"Only the remote-control ones the Parker boys got for Christmas last year."

Noelle drummed her fingers on the helmet. Finally, she turned and glared at Colin. "Did you do this on purpose to get back at me for posting that video of your scuffle at the marketplace?"

Colin huffed. "No, but that's a great idea." He glared back at her. "I asked you nicely not to post that."

"Yes, but I know what my subscribers like, and you don't. I'll have you know that my videos are bringing more people to your little town, which means more money raised for your fundraiser. And that little video of you has gotten tons of *likes*. You should be grateful."

"Grateful? Grateful that you made me look like a fool to my community?"

Noelle turned away. He just didn't get it. She reached in her bag for the scarf and gloves she'd packed. Now that they were sitting still, she realized how cold it was. The wind blew snow in every direction, and her nose felt numb. She cupped her hands against her mouth and blew hot air into the gloves to warm her nose.

Colin gave her a sympathetic look, then took her by the

elbow. "Come on, I know a place where we can get warm."

Noelle looked around. All she could see were unblemished white fields. Thank goodness the snow wasn't deep because they began walking. Colin seemed to know where he was going, so Noelle simply followed behind. Before long, they rounded a hill, and she spotted a cabin in the distance. She never would have found it on her own. "How did you know this was here?" she asked as they drew closer.

"It's an old hunting cabin. Hasn't been used in years."

Noelle sensed there was more to the story, but she kept her questions for later. Now that she knew she'd be warm soon, her attitude improved considerably. Colin reached under the welcome mat, retrieved a key, and opened the front door.

"How did you know the key was there?"

"Everyone knows it's there. If someone gets stuck out here, they're welcome to use the cabin."

"It's your cabin, isn't it?"

Colin shrugged. "Yeah, but I haven't really used it since…" His voice trailed off.

"Aren't you afraid someone will come in and steal things?"

He looked at her and smiled. "You haven't grown up in Evergreen Creek. It's not something we worry about. Most people don't even lock their doors at night. And if someone needs a place to get out of the storm in the middle of winter, I'm more than happy to let them stay here as long as they need to. I keep dry logs by the fireplace and stock the pantry with non-perishables."

Noelle tried to imagine what it was like to live in a place where you didn't have to worry about strangers trespassing on your property. Where people left their hunting lodge available if someone needed to get out of a storm.

She watched Colin add wood to the fireplace and start a fire. Wanting to make herself useful, she went to the kitchen. Opening cabinets, she found packets of hot cocoa mix. She put a pot of water on the stove to boil, rinsed out two cups, then made them each a cup of hot chocolate.

When she returned and handed Colin one of the cups, he thanked her with a grateful smile. He had a nice fire going, so they sat cross-legged in front of the fire, sipping their hot cocoa in comfortable silence.

"This is nice," Noelle said. She stared into the fire, mesmerized by the dancing flames. She couldn't remember the last time she'd simply sat and enjoyed her surroundings without feeling like she should be doing something else.

She looked around the room. It was simple but had a rustic charm, with knotty pine walls and open shelving. She spotted a woman's touch here and there, from the dotted Swiss curtains to the handmade seat cushions.

Noelle grabbed an afghan draped over the back of the couch and wrapped it around her shoulders.

Colin looked at the afghan with a tender smile. "My mother made that."

"Oh."

Noelle moved to take it off, but Colin stopped her. "No, she'd be happy to know it was keeping someone else warm." His gaze moved to the couch. "Some of my happiest memories are sitting here playing games by the fire, my mom sitting on the couch with the afghan draped across her lap."

"What kind of games did you play?" It seemed like the most innocent question she could ask without feeling like she was prying into his memories.

"Depends," he replied. "Mom was a wordsmith. Scrabble was her game. None of us could beat her. Not only did she have an incredible vocabulary, but she had an uncanny knack for finding the highest scoring tiles to complete her words." He smiled at the memory. "She was competitive, but not with other people. She was always competing with herself to get the best score possible."

Noelle could relate. It didn't matter how many subscribers other content creators had on their channel. She wasn't in competition with anyone else. What was important was steadily increasing her own numbers. "I like Scrabble too," she said.

"I'd challenge you to a game, but I think I learned my lesson at the pool table."

It sounded like he was half joking, but for a moment, she regretted the fact that she was leaving after her story here was over. There wouldn't be time for games in front of a roaring fire.

"Now, me and my Dad would have Monopoly marathons," he said. "We'd play for hours while my mother sat on the couch reading a book."

"I'm liking your mother more and more."

Colin nodded. "Everyone loved her. Mom was Mayor of Evergreen Creek for years."

"Really?" That was unexpected.

"Yeah. When she lost her battle with cancer..." He gulped, then continued. "I took her place in the interim. I'd been working beside her, so it wasn't unusual for me to step into what I thought was a temporary situation."

"Not so temporary, huh?"

"I guess I did my job well enough because when the time came, I was elected unanimously. I've been running unopposed since."

"The town must love you."

"I work hard for this town, just like my mother did." It was almost as if he'd forgotten she was there. "According to

Angela, maybe a little too hard. She thinks I should have more of a private life."

"Angela?" Did she feel a tiny stab of jealousy?

"My mom's best friend. She took on the job of being my substitute mother after my mom died. It's not as if I needed a mother, but…"

"Everyone needs a mother, no matter how old you are."

He gave her a searching look, but she wasn't ready to talk about her own family issues. Just because he opened up didn't mean she had to reciprocate.

It couldn't have been more than half an hour later when they heard a snowmobile outside. Noelle was almost sorry that they'd been rescued. She'd been enjoying their time in the cozy cabin, talking about happier days.

When their rescuer took off his helmet and a head of curls tumbled out, Noelle wondered if Geoff was the go-to guy for just about everything in town. Colin handed Noelle her helmet. "Geoff will take you back to the lodge, then he'll come back, and we'll get the other snowmobile going. If not, I'll see you back at the festival later this afternoon."

"Okay, what's on the agenda for this afternoon?"

Colin looked up as if he was searching for the answers on the ceiling. "Umm, the winners of the gingerbread house competition will be announced. A Christmas movie. Oh, and there's the Ugly Sweater Contest."

"You judge who's wearing the ugliest sweater? And you call me mean?"

"Wait until you see the entries. Everyone goes out of their way to have the ugliest sweater imaginable."

"Looking forward to it." She put on her helmet and climbed on Geoff's snowmobile. "See you back in town," she called, waving to Colin.

The sight of him standing in the doorway, backlit by

the firelight, stayed with her all the way back to the lodge. Gretchen met her inside. "So," she said, "how was the reindeer farm? Did one of them have a red nose?"

"Never made it," Noelle said. "Our snowmobile broke down, and we were stranded out in the woods. Geoff had to rescue us."

Gretchen shook her head. "Life here sure is different than what we're used to."

"Yeah. When was the last time I said my snowmobile broke down on the way to the reindeer farm?"

They both had a good laugh about that.

# Chapter Nine

ANGELA STOPPED by Colin's desk. "I hear you were trapped in the cabin with the dragon lady."

"Ah, she's not that bad."

"Oh?" Angela arched an eyebrow.

"Actually, I was thinking about something she said. I may not agree with her method, but her videos are bringing people into town."

"Maybe not in a good way."

"It's good if they're spending money." He stopped and considered. "The better Noelle's videos do, the more people will come to the festival. Noelle said I even have fans among her subscribers."

"Of course. I'm sure they love you."

"Well, if I insert myself into her videos, maybe I can guide the content so she doesn't come off as being so harsh. Then more people will come to town. And the more people who come to the festival, the better chance we have of making our fundraising goals."

Angela gave him a probing look. "I thought you didn't like her?"

"It's not that I don't like her. I just didn't want her bringing any negative publicity to our town. But it seems to be doing just the opposite. The lodge is at full capacity, and every shop in town says business is up." He dipped his head. "Maybe she can be a little abrasive, but…"

Angela grinned. "She's gotten under your skin, hasn't she?"

Had she? Maybe he'd seen a softer side of her when they were trapped together at the cabin. "No," he said with a shake of his head. "My only goal is to make the festival a success. If I have to play along with her little videos, I will."

"And get to spend more time with her," Angela said under her breath.

Colin ignored the dig. This was just for the town's benefit, that's all.

When Angela left, he pulled out his phone. He didn't want Angela to know that he'd already subscribed to Noelle's channel and followed her on social media — only so he could see what she had to say about his town. That was the only reason. But Angela would assume there was an ulterior motive.

He checked Noelle's schedule. She was going to be at the coffee shop next. Well, that was convenient. He stepped out of his office and called to Angela, "I'm going to the coffee shop. I'll be back in an hour."

As Colin neared the coffee shop, he was surprised to see cars everywhere and people lined up on the sidewalk. The crowd parted as he made his way inside to a chorus of greetings.

"Morning, Mayor," the barista called. She gestured to Noelle. "We're about to go live."

"Morning, Katie." He noticed she was wearing make-up and something pink and frilly under her apron.

"You're just in time to join us," Noelle said. She picked up the microphone as Gretchen started the live feed. She turned to the camera and smiled. "This is Noelle Hamilton, and we're here with Katie Flynn, owner and head barista at Evergreen Creek Coffee café, where the locals swear you'll find the best coffee in town." She leaned toward the camera and whispered, "I'm a bit of a coffee snob, and I can attest to that."

She turned to Katie and asked, "So, what makes your coffee so great?"

"Well, we grind the beans fresh daily," Katie said. "And we use only the best beans I can find."

Colin barely listened as they waxed poetic about the flavor of the coffee. It was just coffee, after all. Instead, he watched Noelle as she interviewed the barista. She seemed genuinely interested, and when she smiled, her face lit up with good humor. Why did she have to ruin it with a snippy comment? This time it was something about the best beans being pooped out of some berry-eating bird. He might just give up coffee for good now.

"So what do you think, Mayor?"

"Huh? I like coffee."

She laughed. "A man of few words." She turned to the camera. "This morning, the good Mayor took me to a reindeer farm. I was anxious to show you real live reindeer. But alas, first, our snowmobile broke down in the middle of the woods, and we had to be rescued. Then he came back a few hours later, and we finally drove to the reindeer farm. Turns out it was a dairy farm where the cows wore cheesy reindeer antlers made of brown velvet."

"Who doesn't love cows?" Colin quipped.

The coffee shop crowd laughed.

"I'll admit the reindeer farm is a bit of a joke," Colin added. "I thought you'd get a kick out of it."

Noelle grinned in spite of herself. "So," she said, "I understand you start your day here, conducting business over a cup of Katie Flynn's delicious coffee."

"That's correct."

"You must really love the coffee."

Colin winked at Katie. "I do. And I love the fact that people are more comfortable talking to me over a cup of coffee if they're too intimidated to make an appointment to come into the office."

"Everyone knows they can find him here," Katie said. "He's open for business every morning during his coffee hour." She blushed. "Everyone loves Mayor Colin."

Noelle turned to Colin. "Did you pay her to say that?"

"Do I look like a millionaire?"

She gave him a cool up-and-down glance, from his Caribou boots to his double-quilted flannel jacket. "Maybe a hundredaire."

"You're too generous."

"Generous? Are you hitting me up for a loan?"

His laughter came from deep in his chest, bubbling upward and rumbling in carefree waves. Noelle found it intoxicating. She glanced at Gretchen, who waved her hand, encouraging her to continue.

"So tell us, Mayor. What's on the agenda for today's festivities?"

"Well, there's the Gingerbread House competition."

Noelle rolled her eyes. "Oh, I can't wait."

Colin grinned. "Sorry, it's only for children."

"Darn, I was so looking forward to dipping into a bowl of royal icing." Her voice dripped with sexual innuendo.

His eyes burned into hers, and she could almost see the erotic images flashing through his mind. "I thought you didn't like sweets," he said, his voice a husky growl.

"The question is, do you?"

The air between them sizzled. Noelle wasn't sure how much of it was real and how much was staged for the camera. She took a deep breath to calm her racing heart. Time to get back on track. "So, what else can we look forward to today?"

Colin held her gaze for a moment, then turned to the camera with a winning smile. "Today, we'll announce the winners of the snowmobile parade, followed by Christmas carol karaoke. Then there's the Ugly Sweater Contest."

Noelle glanced at the camera. "According to Colin, ugly is good."

"Yes," Colin said. "In this case, ugly is good." He winked at Noelle. She had no idea what that was all about.

"Then tonight," he said, "we're showing a Christmas movie with complimentary popcorn, then a roaring bonfire with complimentary s'mores." He turned and grinned at her. "What more could a Christmas Grinch ask for?"

Noelle chuckled, then turned to the camera. "So there you have it. Ugly sweaters, Christmas karaoke and s'mores. As the good mayor said, what more can a Christmas Grinch ask for?" She leaned forward and whispered, "I'm pretty sure he's talking about me."

Colin chuckled, then waved goodbye. "See you at the judge's stand to announce the winner of the snowmobile parade."

Noelle was surprised by the flurry of butterflies in her stomach. "Yeah, can't wait," she said with a smirk.

When Colin left, Gretchen pulled Noelle aside. "The live audience was eating it up," she said. "They love the interaction between you and the Mayor."

Noelle swallowed. "Are you suggesting I that should flirt with him?" Somehow, the idea wasn't as distasteful as she thought it would be.

"Well, yeah, but in your own unique way. You know, the sarcasm, the dry wit, the snarkiness."

"I had no idea that was considered flirting."

"Not for most people, but it seems to work with you two." Gretchen turned her screen to Noelle. She'd rewound the video to the part where Noelle and Colin started talking, and the screen lit up with hearts and stars and … donations! Well, wasn't that interesting.

"I guess I can take one for the team," she said. "If it brings our ratings up, then everyone is happy."

After leaving the coffee shop, Noelle and Gretchen made their rounds of the marketplace. Then, they filmed some of the children at the gingerbread house workshop. The kids were covered with icing. More spice drops and chocolate chips ended up in their mouths than on their gingerbread houses.

A bubbly blonde girl of about five offered Noelle a sticky chunk of gingerbread covered with M&M's.

Noelle bent down to the child's height and took a tiny nibble. "Mmmm."

"I made it myself," the little girl said.

"You did a great job. Maybe you'll be a famous baker when you grow up."

"Or a princess."

Noelle gave the girl a hug. "You can be whatever you want to be," she said. "A baker, a princess, or a firefighter. It's all up to you."

She stood up and smiled as the little girl went back to decorating her gingerbread blob.

Gretchen turned off the camera. "That was sweet."

"I don't do sweet," Noelle said. "Just ask Colin."

After a busy morning, Noelle finally made it to the judge's stand. She was surprised to see that Colin had saved her a spot beside him. He'd even thought to lay a blanket over the cold metal bleacher seat.

"Where's Gretchen?" he asked.

"Oh, she's off on her own for a few hours."

"You're not going live again?"

"Nope. I'll take some shots of the top three, then close-ups of the winner. Those will go into a montage of some of the other events. Like the gingerbread house workshop. We got some nice footage there today."

"Don't forget Christmas carol karaoke." His grin widened. "Perhaps you'd like to get on the karaoke schedule?"

"Shoot me now."

"Ah, come on. I bet you do a killer rendition of 'It's Raining Men.'"

"More like *snowing* men."

"Ha!"

Why did she find it so satisfying to make him laugh? She shivered, and he leaned close. The heat from his body took some of the chill off.

"Here come the finalists," he said.

Noelle turned on her camera and started recording clips of the top five finalists. She'd get close-ups of the winners after they were announced. For now, she was only interested in a few shots to add to the winter festival collage.

Colin leaned closer, and she welcomed the heat from his body. He handed her a piece of paper and then spoke into the microphone. "Here to announce our winner is Noelle Hamilton from Your Social Media Source."

Noelle was caught off guard but took the microphone and started reading off the finalists. "And the winner is," she took a dramatic pause, "*The Polar Express*, decorated by

Jim and Judy Tremain of Cedar Ridge Road. Congratulations!"

The crowd roared, and Colin stepped down from the judge's stand to retrieve a trophy, which he presented to the winners. Noelle missed his warmth already. It made her uncomfortable to realize how much she looked forward to sitting beside him. Rather than confront it, she packed up her camera and slipped away before he noticed she was gone.

She picked up a salad on the way back to the lodge. It was large enough to share with Gretchen, but her assistant wasn't in her room. Probably out with Geoff. At least one of them was having a good time.

It was hard to concentrate on her work. She picked at her salad but found herself wondering what everyone was doing at the festival. She checked her watch. There was time to make it for the Christmas carol karaoke. Turning off her computer, she decided to head back to the festival. It wouldn't hurt to get some more footage, she told herself. But the truth was, she felt lonely. She missed the excitement, the camaraderie, and maybe, just maybe, she missed Colin.

She made her way to the community hall and was drawn to the room where the karaoke was being held. The sound of music and laughter was hard to miss. She took a seat at the back of the auditorium and watched.

She recognized the person on stage as Bubba of the pie-eating contest. He'd obviously recovered because he was dancing and gyrating to an off-key rendition of "Rockin' Around the Christmas Tree." What he lacked in musical ability, he more than made up for with his dance moves.

Next up was an entire family wearing matching reindeer sweaters and antler headbands who performed

"Rudolph the Red-Nosed Reindeer," followed by three young boys singing "Frosty the Snowman." When a little girl started singing "All I Want For Christmas is My Two Front Teeth" while pointing to the gap in her own teeth, Noelle couldn't help but smile. She caught sight of Gretchen in the front row filming.

Next up was one of the cousins. She couldn't remember their names, but it was the one who made the chocolate cocoa mixes. He started singing "Jingle Bells," but when he got to the chorus, he pointed the microphone at the crowd, who yelled back, "...laughing all the way." It went on like that for several rounds, but even Noelle participated and started singing the chorus back.

This went on for hours. Even Colin got into the act with a version of "You're a Mean One, Mr. Grinch," obviously directed at her. Then Geoff took the stage with a loud and raucous rendition of "Grandma Got Run Over by a Reindeer."

Noelle shook her head as the crowd whooped and hollered. Whatever possessed people who were entirely tone-deaf to get up in front of an audience and sing loud and off-key? They were terrible — but also were having such a good time forgetting the lyrics and laughing. Maybe it wasn't about the performance after all. Maybe it was all about just having fun and not taking life so seriously.

She caught up with Colin when the karaoke ended. "Nice choice of songs," she said.

He grinned. "It's one of my favorites."

"And why is that?"

He stopped to think about it. "I guess because in the end, the Grinch's heart grows bigger, and he's surrounded by people who care about him. He discovers the spirit of Christmas that he's denied all along."

"So you like happy endings."

"Yeah. Don't you?"

She had to stop and think about his question. In her experience, there were no neat and tidy, happy-ending wrap-ups. Life was a series of ups and downs, wins and losses. "Life isn't like the movies," she said.

The look he gave her was hard to decipher. Compassion? Pity? Did he think everyone saw the world through rose-colored glasses? Yeah, maybe she was a bit cynical, but it prepared her for the hard knocks of life. Being eternally optimistic only sets you up for a letdown.

But looking at his clear, trusting eyes, she wondered if maybe there was a way to meet in the middle.

Colin snapped his fingers. "I almost forgot. I have a present for you." He made a gesture for her to wait. "I'll be right back."

He returned with a package wrapped in tissue and handed it to her.

She unwrapped the tissue and peered inside. "Oh no. Nope, not gonna happen."

"Come on, be a good sport."

She held up a flaming red sweater with dangling green tassels and silver jingle bells. A life-sized Grinch face was appliqued on the front of the sweater. The sleeves and collar were trimmed in white faux fur. "This is the ugliest sweater I've ever seen," she said.

"Then you're sure to win. And considering how competitive you are, I was sure you'd jump at the chance."

How was she going to save face? It was almost as if he was determined to embarrass her. But she'd be damned if she let him get the upper hand. "What time does it start?"

He checked his watch. "You have half an hour."

"I'll be there," she said. But first, she needed to run back to the lodge. She remembered packing a pair of green leggings that would go perfect with this sweater. If she was going to do this, she planned to go all out.

She changed quickly, then made her way back to the school auditorium in time to line up with the other ugly sweaters — and it was a long, long line of ugly sweaters! She stopped in front of the judge's stand, then turned to Gretchen's camera and struck a pose.

Colin stood at the sidelines, smiling at her. Noelle felt vindicated. He didn't think she'd do it. Well, she showed him she could be a good sport as well. Besides, he was right. She was competitive enough to want to win, even if winning meant she had the ugliest sweater of all.

The sweater wearers lined up on one side of the auditorium while the judges consulted their scores. Then, the announcements began. Colin stood holding a stack of scorecards and a microphone. "In third place is Amanda Kingsley."

Amanda stepped forward. Her sweater was strung with twinkling LED lights. She looked like a walking Christmas tree. A nearby table erupted in applause as her friends congratulated her. She accepted her ribbon and joined them at their table.

"In second place," Colin said, "is Bubba Brown."

Bubba's sweater had a giant reindeer on the front with a blinking red nose. He ran up and grabbed the ribbon from Colin, holding it over his head and dancing in a victory march. The crowd laughed and applauded.

"And in first place," Colin paused dramatically, then glanced at Noelle. "The Grinch herself, Noelle Hamilton."

The entire auditorium broke out in cheers. Noelle noticed Gretchen was still filming as Colin nudged the microphone in her face. "How does it feel to be the ugliest?"

"I beg your pardon?"

He laughed. "Ugliest sweater, that is."

She laughed along with him. "Any win is a good win."

"Well, you're always a winner in our book, right, everyone?" He encouraged the crowd, who stood on their feet and applauded.

As hard as she tried not to let it go to her head, she couldn't help feeling proud. It was a silly, ugly sweater contest. Not exactly something to put on her resume.

But the way Colin was smiling at her made it all worthwhile.

# Chapter Ten

THAT EVENING, Noelle and Gretchen put their heads together, choosing which pictures to add to the video collage. Definitely the snowmobile parade and a few from the gingerbread workshop, which were actually kind of cute. She had some adorable shots of kids covered in icing and swiping decorating candy to shove in their mouths when no one was looking.

There was some painful video of karaoke night. But everyone was having such a good time that Noelle didn't have the heart to make fun of them. Maybe she was growing soft.

"Not a problem. The Ugly Sweater Contest is the cherry on the cake."

Then, it was all worthwhile. "How are our numbers looking?" she asked.

Gretchen pulled up her spreadsheet. "Fabulous. The viewers love it when you and Colin interact. Every time he makes an appearance, people go crazy."

"Hmm…" Guess she'd have to *interact* more with Mr.

Popularity. Not that she hated the thought. If only he wasn't so gung-ho about everything Christmas.

"Honestly," Gretchen said, "the marketplace clip with Colin and the cousins fighting is still our most watched video."

"Maybe I can get him to beat up an old lady next."

"Or kick a dog."

"Better yet, kick a reindeer."

Gretchen laughed. "Yeah, but not one of those fake reindeer cows."

Noelle shut everything down and rubbed her eyes. "That's enough for tonight. What do you say we knock back a few at Blitzen's?"

"Sounds like a plan."

Half an hour later, they entered the cozy bar. The walls were adorned with festive decorations, red and green garland, and icicle lights. Cheery holiday music played in the background. They found two empty chairs at the bar and settled in. Noelle reviewed the craft beer list and ordered an IPA while Gretchen settled for a rum runner. It felt good to relax and not talk about all things Christmas.

"So, what do you think of the festival so far?" Gretchen asked.

Noelle sighed. "I think it's about four days too long, for one thing."

Gretchen nodded. "But it's a big deal and their biggest fundraising activity for the year." She tapped her fingers on the edge of her glass. "At least the Mayor is involved. He has his hand in everything to make it a success."

Noelle noticed a woman two chairs away at the bar, watching them intently. Considering how much the Mayor was loved around town, she'd have to watch what she said.

"He's quite the charmer, though, wouldn't you say?"

Noelle shrugged. "I haven't noticed."

"Seems to me there's a bit of chemistry between the two of you."

"That's just for the camera. You said the viewers loved it when we interacted. So I'm interacting." She shook her head. "I just don't get why Colin is so gung-ho over Christmas. It's only one day a year."

The lady at the end of the bar leaned over. "I can answer that for you." She gestured to the empty seat beside Noelle. "May I?"

Noelle nodded.

The woman reached out her hand. "I'm Angela Cooper."

Noelle took her outstretched hand. "I'm Noelle, and this is my assistant Gretchen."

"Nice to meet you," she said. "I couldn't help but overhear your conversation. I know you're covering the festival, so if there's any backstory I can give you, I'd be happy to." She smiled. "Colin's mother, Eva, was my best friend. I've known him since he was in diapers."

Oh, so this was the Angela that Colin had talked about. "Colin told me his mother died."

Angela nodded. "I've tried to take her place in Colin's life, but I had some big shoes to fill. Colin told you she was the previous mayor, right?"

Noelle nodded.

"Everyone loved her. And she loved Christmas. It was her favorite holiday. She had a big open house every year and invited the whole town. Eva was essentially the Christmas spirit of Evergreen Creek."

Noelle couldn't help but compare this idyllic image of Christmas to her own sad memories. She envied Colin's growing up surrounded by friends and family. "So, he does all this to keep his mother's memory alive?"

"Well," Angela replied. "There's more to it than that."

Her eyes grew misty. "The year the mill closed down, Eva lost her battle with cancer. Colin became interim mayor and struggled to save the town. We were headed for financial ruin when Colin came up with the idea of having a Christmas festival to raise money. Everyone in town jumped in to help plan and run it." She laughed. "We made some mistakes along the way, but we raised enough money to keep the town running for another year. And each year, the festival gets bigger and better." Her eyes glowed with pride. "We owe it all to Colin."

"And that's why he takes it so personally."

Angela nodded. "And that's why he puts in long hours every day to make it a success."

Noelle felt a stab of regret for all her trash-talking. Colin's intensity made more sense now. It was too bad she didn't share his love of all things Christmas.

Angela stood to leave. "I'll leave you two to your business. Just remember," she said, "this is more than a job to Colin. It's a way to keep his mother's legacy alive."

Noelle nodded, seeing Colin in a new light through Angela's eyes.

When the woman left, she turned to Gretchen. "What do you think?"

Gretchen drummed her fingernails on the counter. "I think what we're doing, whether people here approve or not, is good for the town. The lodge is filled with tourists, the local shops are seeing increased revenue and attendance at the festival is way up."

"So you don't think I should start sugarcoating things?"

"I think what you're doing is working. You know what they say. If it ain't broke…"

Still, Noelle wondered if she was doing right by Angela, Colin, and his mother's memory.

It was a question she continued to ask herself as she

tossed and turned in bed that night. Had she let her own feelings about Christmas influence her reports? Maybe if she'd had the fairytale Christmas holidays the townspeople all seemed to enjoy, she'd be more holly jolly about the celebration.

She sat up and grabbed her phone, knowing her mother would still be up since it was three hours earlier on the West Coast. Her mother answered on the second ring. "Noelle? Is everything all right?"

Noelle felt a twinge of guilt, realizing she called so rarely that her mother assumed something bad happened. "Nothing wrong. I just wanted to wish you a Merry Christmas."

"Well, Merry Christmas to you, dear. What are your plans this year?"

"I hadn't given it much thought."

"You know you're always welcome here. I could send you a plane ticket if you want to visit over the holidays."

She could buy her own plane ticket, but it was nice of her mother to offer. Not as if she had any intention of flying to Portland, Oregon over the holidays. Or ever, for that matter.

"We never really spent much time together over Christmas, did we?" Noelle asked. "I was with Grandpa."

Her mother's voice softened. "That's what you wanted. You begged me to let you stay with him. I was working two jobs just to survive, and it seemed like the best option. He adored you."

Was that regret she heard in her mother's voice? Noelle didn't remember begging to stay with her grandfather. Still, in all the turmoil of the nasty fights and divorce, her grandfather's house felt like a safe haven. Any young girl would have preferred that to her own home.

Her mother's voice broke. "I should have insisted you

stay with me, but I took the easy way out, and I'm sorry. I'm sorry you felt abandoned, and I'm sorry for all the years we missed being together."

Noelle wiped a tear from her eye. "We can't make up for those lost years," she said. "But maybe we can start today to make new memories."

"I would love that." There were tears in her mother's voice as well.

They talked about Noelle's job. She was surprised that her mother had watched every episode so far. They caught up on everything, from her mother's partner and their new home to her job in real estate. When they hung up, Noelle laid back on her pillow and instantly fell asleep.

# Chapter Eleven

As soon as Colin walked into the office the next morning, he saw the look on Angela's face and knew there was trouble ahead. "What now?"

Angela gave him a thin-lipped smile. "The people running the sausage and pepper stand are having car trouble and running really late."

"Damn, damn, damn." What else could go wrong? "Can we…?"

Angela stopped him before he could finish. "I've called everyone, and there's no one else available."

"Of course. It's foodie night, so everyone who can cook already has their own stand."

"And those who aren't cooking are working other events today."

Colin rolled up his sleeves. "Guess that leaves me."

Angela patted him on the shoulder. "Good luck."

Colin made his way to the food truck. He wasn't much of a cook, but he enjoyed grilling on the weekend. How hard could it be?

Looking around inside the truck, he was grateful to see

it was stocked with all the ingredients he needed — bags of peppers, onions, hoagie rolls, and packages of sausage in the refrigerator. He grabbed an apron, pulled it over his head, then turned on the grill.

Where to start?

He leaned over to grab a cutting board and burned his wrist on the grill. Damn. Not off to a good start. He opened a cabinet drawer and found a knife big enough to be called a machete, at least in his mind. He was no knife expert.

He threw some sausage on the grill, grabbed the machete, and started cutting onions. His eyes teared up, and he made the mistake of wiping them with his hand and getting onion juice in his eyes. He spent the next five minutes washing his eyes out with a wet dishrag. Finally able to see again, he chopped peppers and added them to the onions on the grill.

A line began forming, and sweat broke out on his forehead. "I'll be right with you," he called. "Just give me a minute." He quickly threw a sausage on a roll, then covered it with peppers and onions. He handed it to the customer and took his payment.

Before he could even make a change, the customer held up his sandwich and complained, "This sausage isn't cooked all the way through."

"Oh, I'm so sorry. Here, give it to me, and I'll make a new one." This time, he cut into the sausage to be sure it was cooked before making another sandwich. He must have done something right because the customer walked off without another complaint. One down. He wasn't sure how he'd get through the rest of the day. He had a burn on his wrist, a cut on his finger bandaged with a Mickey Mouse band-aid, and his eyes still stung from the onions.

As if things couldn't get any worse, he saw Noelle

walking toward the stand. Just what he needed. More sarcasm and more embarrassing videos. She watched him struggle, then instead of taking advantage of his ineptitude, she came around, climbed into the food truck, grabbed an apron, and started working beside him.

"I used to work in food service in college," she said. "I know how much it sucks to be in the weeds."

"Thank you," he said. He couldn't begin to express how grateful he was. She began cutting the vegetables without asking. "How can you cut onions without tearing up?"

"Trade secret." She smiled and held up a wet paper towel. "Put the wet towel near the onion. I'm not sure how it works. It's something about the chemicals in the onion being drawn to the wet towel instead of the moisture in your eyes. I don't know why, just that it works."

"Well, you learn something new every day."

She tossed the onions on the grill and then started slicing the peppers. They worked efficiently as a team, cooking, serving sausage sandwiches, and collecting money hand over fist. Colin wiped the sweat from his forehead. He glanced over and noticed the steam made Noelle's hair curl around her face. She looked younger, less stern, and more approachable. Every now and then, Colin would catch her shaking her head and chuckling. "What?"

She pointed to his apron. "Did you pick that out?"

"No, I just grabbed it off that hook over there. Why?"

She reached forward and traced the words across his chest.

He looked down, and even upside down, he could see what the words spelled out — *Kiss the Cook*. He couldn't help but laugh. "I should be the one kissing you. You saved my butt back there." He grew somber. "Seriously. Thank you."

She nodded, then turned away as if embarrassed. Before things could get uncomfortable, the staff hired to run the sausage and pepper stand arrived, full of apologies. Colin was just grateful to hand over the apron to someone else. His hand brushed against her shoulder when he helped Noelle out of her apron. "I owe you dinner," he said.

"Anything but sausage and peppers," she replied.

"I hear you. Unfortunately, I have a full schedule here right now, but I promise I'll take you to a nice steak house when the festival ends."

"I don't need an expensive dinner," she said.

"In that case…" He gestured to different food trucks as they walked. "We have our choice of shish kabob, fried dough, blooming onion, pizza…"

Noelle's eyes lit up. "Pizza?"

Colin grinned. "A girl after my own heart."

FOR SOME REASON, Colin's words made Noelle's knees go weak. Maybe she was just weak with hunger. The pizza was hot and spicy, with just the right amount of bend, as good as any slice she could get in the city. "Not bad," she said, taking another bite.

"I'm impressed," Colin said. "Usually, people from the city think they can't get a decent slice anywhere else."

"Well, we are the pizza experts."

They carried their food and drinks to a picnic table beneath a tent. The cool air felt good after being inside the hot sausage truck. Their knees touched beneath the table, and she didn't pull away. After working so closely together in the food truck, it felt natural being this close.

"We made a good team back there," Colin said as if reading her thoughts.

"It was no big deal."

"Maybe so, but I still owe you a steak dinner when this is over."

She didn't bother to remind him that she was only here for the festival. Once it was over, she'd be going home. There wouldn't be time for a steak dinner or anything else. Instead, she asked him about the fundraising efforts. "Do you think you'll meet your goal?"

Colin shrugged. "God willing, and the creek don't rise."

Noelle nearly choked on her last bite of pizza.

Colin shot her a questioning look.

"My grandfather used to say that all the time," she explained. "I don't think I've ever heard anyone else use that phrase." Her eyes stung as she held back tears. "He was the greatest man I ever knew."

Colin reached out and covered her hand with his. He didn't press for more information. Just let her know he was there if she needed to talk.

"He raised me after my parents divorced," she said. Looking back on those years, she realized how much of a toll it must have taken on him. She was angry, bitter, and resentful. That, on top of the normal teenage angst, must have been a lot to take. But he'd been there, unlike her own parents. He was the one person she could count on, no matter how rebellious she acted. "I miss him," she murmured.

She took a deep breath and sat up straight. No feeling sorry for herself. No showing weakness. That was one lesson she'd learned growing up. If she wanted to be taken seriously, she had to develop a tough exterior.

She scooped up her napkins and tossed them in the

trash. "Thanks for the pizza," she said, then turned to leave.

"Hey," he called after her. "Will you be back later for the afternoon events?"

"Wouldn't miss them for the world." But for now, she needed to get away. Her emotions were too close to the surface, and the urge to open up to Colin was too tempting.

Back in her room, she checked the files and was surprised to see that Gretchen had uploaded a clip from when she and Colin were working together in the food truck. Noelle hadn't even seen her filming. Was it any wonder? She'd been so caught up in their working to get the food cooked and served she hadn't had time for anything else.

Gretchen had captured the moment when Noelle traced the words on Colin's apron. *Kiss the Cook.* The way they were looking at each other, it almost seemed for a moment she would. Anyone watching would think there was something romantic going on. Of course, there wasn't.

Noelle watched the video with awe. When she turned away from him, Colin stared at her with an undeniable attraction. His gaze softened, and his lips turned up in a half smile. And then … Noelle was mortified. When Colin turned, she gave him a lecherous stare, top to bottom, with a definite focus on his bottom.

He'd made a comment about her saving his butt. That's probably why she'd looked at his. Yeah, that was her excuse. But when she saw the feed, she noticed there were several comments about her checking him out. Like Gretchen said, the viewers loved the interaction, which explained why she'd been so quick to upload it.

Noelle let out a deep sigh. Faking a connection with Colin was becoming far too easy to do.

Her phone vibrated, and she pulled it out of her pocket to see a text message from Colin.

*It's a shame you missed the Grinch movie last night. I think tonight's movie will be more to your liking. It's a classic. I'll save you a spot.*

HER HEART RACED. Should she go? She'd avoided sappy Christmas movies her entire life. Did she want to watch one sitting beside Mr. Christmas himself?

Before she could decide what to do, Gretchen popped her head in the door. "What do you think?"

"I think..." She tried to come up with something that made sense. Her emotions were all over the place. "I think the viewers loved it, like you said."

"So, you like my idea of incorporating more flirting between you and Colin?"

"*Like* is an overstatement. I'll tolerate it."

Gretchen giggled. "Seems to me you were doing more than tolerating him at the sausage grill."

Somehow, she made the word *sausage* sound suggestive. Or maybe, Noelle thought, it was just her own dirty mind.

"Are you going to the movie tonight?" Gretchen asked.

"Haven't decided. You?"

"Yeah, Geoff asked me to join him."

"Sounds like a date. Are things getting serious between you two?"

Gretchen blushed. "I like him. He's fun to be around."

"We'll only *be around* a few more days."

Gretchen shrugged. "I'll worry about that later. For now, I'm having a fabulous time."

Noelle hoped it was simply an innocent flirtation. She

didn't want to have to hire a new assistant if Gretchen decided to plant roots here in Evergreen Creek.

Rather than make a hasty decision, Noelle decided to stroll around town, taking candid shots along the way. She discovered a darling independent bookstore, always one of her favorite places to spend time. She wandered the aisles, touching books, inhaling the scent of paper and ink. She found a notebook she couldn't resist buying despite having dozens of notebooks at home. It was an addiction.

The owner recognized her right away. "Oh, Noelle Hamilton! I've been watching your videos," she gushed. "I have to thank you. We've had more customers this week than in the previous month. It's been amazing."

"You're welcome. But I can't take all the credit. Books make great Christmas gifts." She placed a stack of books on the counter and took out her credit card.

"Are these gifts? I can wrap them for you if you'd like."

"No. Actually, they're for me."

"Really?" The owner tipped her head and gave Noelle a keen stare. "You strike me as someone who prefers audio-books or ebooks."

"Oh, I love downloading ebooks to my e-reader as well. But I can't resist adding a paper book to my collection."

"A story is a story, right?"

Noelle handed over her credit card. "Right."

Leaving the store with her purchases, Noelle made her way to a boho boutique, where she found a hand-knit slouch hat she knew Gretchen would love. She couldn't wait to see her open it. This hand-picked gift would be in sharp contrast to the impersonal gift card she usually gave her assistant over the holidays.

At the last minute, Noelle decided to go to the movie. She figured if it was cheesy enough, she could find plenty to make fun of. It was a short walk to the school. The movie "theater" was a projector and large screen in the school auditorium.

She spotted Colin immediately. He must have been staring at the auditorium door because he waved and gestured to the empty seat beside him as soon as he saw her. He balanced a cardboard bucket of popcorn on his lap.

When Noelle joined him, his face broke out in a wide smile, and before she could stop herself, she smiled back. When she sat, their thighs touched, and a shiver of heat worked up her spine. But she didn't pull away. All around them, people were making small talk while waiting for the movie to start. But Noelle felt like she and Colin were in their own private little bubble.

Colin leaned close, his voice a whisper against her cheek. "What's your favorite Christmas movie?" he asked.

"I don't have a favorite. To be honest, I can't remember ever watching a Christmas movie."

He looked at her as if she'd just kissed a frog. "I can't believe you've never seen a Christmas movie."

Noelle shrugged. "Maybe when I was five or six. Something about a dancing snowman or something."

He stared at her for a second, and she wasn't sure if she saw surprise or pity on his face, but he didn't push for an explanation. "Well, this one is a classic. I'm surprised you've never seen it. It's called *It's a Wonderful Life.*"

"Sounds ... wonderful." It actually sounded cheesy to her, but that could work in her favor. It didn't matter how many hearts and likes she got when she was interacting with Colin. Her trademark was saying the things other people were thinking, no matter how sarcastic or snarky. She wasn't about to lose her edge, no matter how charming Colin might be.

She lost count of how many people came by to say

hello or chat for a few minutes with Colin. "Do you know *everybody* in town?" she asked.

"I grew up here," he said.

That didn't totally explain it. Sure, he was the mayor, and he'd grown up in this small town, but it was more than that. People sought him out. They were genuinely happy to see him. And he treated everyone like a close friend. Noelle had a pretty good bullshit detector. She'd know if it was all an act. It wasn't. He was just one of those good guys who everyone gravitated toward.

The movie started, and she sat back to watch. When Colin said it was a classic, he obviously meant it was made a thousand years ago. It was even in black and white.

As if reading her thoughts, Colin leaned over and whispered, "They colorized the film years later, but I think the original black-and-white version is more charming."

*Charming.* She couldn't think of anyone she'd ever known who called anything charming, let alone an old movie. But it didn't take long for her to stop thinking about Colin and concentrate on the movie. She was hooked. She sat forward in her seat, engrossed in the story. When it came to the line that "no man is a failure who has friends," she glanced at Colin. He looked over, and she smiled. It was as if that line was written just for him.

Embarrassed, she looked away and reached into the popcorn bucket. Colin reached in at the same time, and their fingers brushed. It might have been accidental, or he may have done it on purpose. Either way, it sent a tingle straight to her center. Who knew buttery fingers could be so erotic? She held his gaze and brought a popcorn kernel to her mouth. His gaze followed the movement as she opened her lips, touched the kernel with the tip of her tongue, and then brought it into her mouth.

Was she flirting with him? And the camera wasn't even on them.

She turned away, feeling the heat rise to her cheeks. The place where their thighs touched generated warmth as if the two of them had set off a chemical reaction. She turned back to the screen, ignoring the heat of his gaze.

When the movie was over, she couldn't move for a few minutes.

"Well, what did you think?" he asked as the room emptied.

She didn't want to admit how much the movie had touched her. It would spoil her image. "I can see why it's a classic."

He smiled as if he could see right through her. "I'll give you a list of other classic Christmas movies you haven't seen so you can catch up on lost time."

She liked that he didn't ask why she hadn't watched this or any other Christmas movie. Maybe that's why she felt she could tell him about it. Not right now, but when the time was right.

Gretchen met Noelle and Colin outside the auditorium. "I had a great idea," she said. "I talked to Cynthia Coughlin about doing a one-on-one craft class, and she agreed. It will be an extra bonus for our Patreon subscribers."

Noelle nodded. "Sure, sounds great."

"So you and Colin will be up for that?"

Noelle glanced at Colin. He shrugged one shoulder. "I guess if it brings more publicity to the festival, I can do something crafty."

Noelle wasn't sure but trusted Gretchen's instincts. "Okay, then I'm in as well."

"Great. I'll confirm with Cynthia. Is ten o'clock tomorrow morning okay with you guys?"

Noelle and Colin both agreed. Noelle could see what Gretchen was up to. One more opportunity to throw the two of them together for the viewers. Okay, she'd take one for the team as long as Colin was up for it.

She turned to leave, but Colin stopped her. "This may sound weird," he said. "But Angela asked us to come over for dinner. I've been putting her off for weeks because I've had so much to do, but she insists. Says I work too hard."

Noelle couldn't help but smile. "That's a motherly thing to say." It was bittersweet, coming on the heels of her conversation with her own mother. Then it hit her. "Us? Me and you?"

He nodded. "Yeah. Would you mind?"

Noelle blinked. She couldn't think of a single reason Angela would invite her along with Colin, but to decline her invitation would be an insult, not only to Angela but to Colin as well. "Sure," she said. "I'd be honored."

The look of relief on his face was evident. "Thanks, it'll mean a lot to her."

"What time?"

Colin glanced at his watch. "Now?"

Noelle was flustered. She'd never been invited to meet someone's family or Angela's relationship with Colin was. Family friend? Mother substitute? "Shouldn't I pick up flowers or a bottle of wine or something?"

Colin shook his head and smiled. "Nope, just bring yourself." He shuffled his feet. "Well, technically, *I'll* be bringing you, but you know what I mean."

Noelle looked around and realized they were the last to leave. When Colin held out his arm, she followed suit, and together they walked to his car. He held the door open for her, and for once, she didn't feel the need to inform him she could open her own door as she'd done with past dates. He knew she could open her own door, but she could see that chivalry had been bred into him in the same way he used *please* and *thank you* to everyone without hesitation. There was no ulterior motive or superior attitude. He was simply being a gentleman.

Once she was belted inside, he came around to the driver's side and started the ignition. "Angela is the sweetest, kindest woman you'll ever meet," he said. "But, and how do I put this? She does speak her mind. If she disagrees with you, you'll know it. If she wants something from you, she'll tell you. She's very direct." His brow creased into a thoughtful motion. "Now that I think of it," he added, "she's a lot like you."

"Well, that's a high compliment." She grinned. "I think."

"Oh, it is. You'll love her."

Noelle debated whether to tell Colin she'd already met Angela. In the end, she decided it was better to be upfront about it. "I've already met her," she said. "I was at Blitzen's with Gretchen, discussing the festival. I might have commented about why it was such a big deal." She cleared her throat. "Or something like that."

He chuckled. "Why doesn't that surprise me?"

"Well, if it's any consolation, Angela overheard me and jumped to your defense."

"Also, no surprise there."

"She told me how important it was to keep your mother's legacy alive and how hard you work to keep the town solvent."

He nodded, but instead of expanding on the conversation, he announced they'd arrived. He pulled the car in front of a single-story ranch with a wide front porch. A festive holiday wreath adorned the front door, and fairy lights twinkled along the porch railing.

Angela greeted them at the door. "I saw you pull up," she said.

Noelle wondered if she'd been standing by the window waiting.

Angela hugged Colin in greeting and then turned to Noelle with outstretched arms. Noelle stood frozen. She wasn't much of a hugger. Or toucher, for that matter. She started to step forward, then stopped. Angela gave her a look of complete understanding and waited. Then Noelle stepped forward and allowed herself to be embraced.

"There, was that so hard?" Angela murmured in her ear. Surprisingly, it wasn't. As a matter of fact, Noelle was sorry when the hug ended.

Angela gestured for them to come inside. The living room was cozy, with candles on the mantel surrounded by greenery. A six-foot tree covered in ornaments and tinsel commanded the corner of the room. Noelle took a deep breath of the crisp pine scent. "Is that a real tree?"

"Of course. Fresh from Dolan's Tree Farm up the road a piece." She took Colin's arm as they moved to the living room. "I have Colin to thank for it. He cuts down a tree for me every Christmas."

"Where else am I going to put your presents?" he said with a smile.

Noelle was fascinated by their interaction. It was teasing and loving at the same time. If Angela was a substitute mother to Colin, Noelle couldn't imagine what it must have been like growing up with his real mother. And how much it must have hurt to lose her.

"Can I get you a glass of wine?" Angela asked. "I have soda, cider, and hot chocolate as well."

For some reason, sitting beside a fully lit Christmas tree with "Silent Night" playing softly in the background, Noelle felt a sudden urge for hot chocolate. Maybe it was a throwback to her early childhood, or maybe Christmas Town was rubbing off on her. "I'll have hot chocolate, please."

"Me too," Colin said. "Extra whipped cream."

Noelle started to stand. "Can I help?"

Angela waved her away. "No, dear. I have it."

When Angela went into the kitchen, Colin turned to Noelle. "Good choice," he said. "She makes the best hot chocolate around. None of that packaged cocoa mix. She uses fresh milk and chocolate. And some secret ingredient that brings it over the top. You'll see."

Colin was right. When Angela returned, she carried a tray of mugs filled with steaming hot chocolate, whipped cream, and marshmallows. She set the tray down, and Colin took over, like some kind of hot chocolate sommelier, scooping marshmallows, adding whipped cream and a dash of cinnamon, then stirring it all with a candy cane stick. If Noelle wasn't diabetic now, surely this mug of pure sugar would send her over the edge.

But wow, was it delicious. The three of them wore whipped cream mustaches that set them all giggling. Colin reached for a Christmas cookie on a red and green platter. "Just one before dinner," Angela said. "You'll ruin your appetite." It sounded like something she'd said many times before.

Noelle felt more relaxed than she had in a long time. She wondered what it would have been like to grow up with a family that cut down Christmas trees every year and made hot chocolate from scratch. Maybe she'd have a better outlook on life.

A timer sounded in the kitchen. "Dinner's ready," Angela said. They followed her into the dining room, where she set out plates of comfort food — meatloaf, mashed potatoes, green beans, and fried apples.

The combined aromas made Noelle's mouth water. Everything was delicious. The meatloaf was moist and well-seasoned. The potatoes were light and fluffy. She even went back for seconds on the green beans. She'd been living on takeout; this was the first home-cooked meal she'd had in … she didn't know how long.

When they finished, Noelle sat back and rubbed her tummy. "That was incredible. I can't remember the last time I ate like that."

"Glad you enjoyed it," Angela said with a hint of pride. "You're welcome anytime." She started picking up plates. "I plan on wrapping up some meatloaf for Colin to take home to make meatloaf sandwiches. Can I make you a dish?"

Noelle shook her head. "No, thank you. I don't have a refrigerator in my room."

"And how are you enjoying your stay at the lodge?" Angela asked while they cleared the dishes.

"It's very nice. And most everything is within walking distance, which is convenient."

Colin piped in. "If not, I can always give you a ride on the snowmobile." His eyebrows rose and fell comically, making the suggestion sound suggestive.

"No, thank you."

Noelle rinsed the dishes, and Colin loaded them into the dishwasher while Angela packed up the leftovers and prepared a container of leftovers for Colin. It seemed like she'd done this many times before. Considering she claimed Colin worked too hard, she probably also worried he didn't eat right.

"How often does she feed you?" Noelle asked.

"Once or twice a week. She promised my mother she'd take care of me, and she takes her promises seriously." He gazed across the room and smiled. "It helps that I enjoy being with her. She's the closest thing I have to home."

Noelle nodded thoughtfully. What felt like home for her? The office? Her apartment? She hadn't invested enough of herself into either of those places. She looked around. It was more than the decorations and hot chocolate that made Angela's house a home. It was the fact that she filled it with love and memories.

Before they left, Angela added a package of cookies to Colin's take-home bag and whispered, "For my cookie monster."

Colin laughed and leaned over to kiss her forehead. "Thanks again. See you at the office tomorrow."

"The office?" Noelle asked as they got back in Colin's car.

"Angela is the treasurer on the Board. We share office space."

"Oh." Somehow, Noelle had missed that little fact. No wonder Angela had invited her to dinner. She had as much riding on the festival's success as Colin did.

<h1 style="text-align:center">Chapter Twelve</h1>

THE NEXT MORNING, Gretchen knocked on Noelle's door to remind her about the craft lesson she'd agreed to do for their viewers. To Noelle's surprise, the craft lesson was taking place at Cynthia Coughlin's house. She and Gretchen walked the two blocks over to Cynthia's house. Noelle groaned when she saw the front yard covered with blow-up reindeer, elves, and Santa on his sleigh. Twinkling lights outlined the entire house; of course, the centerpiece was a brightly lit and decorated Christmas tree in the front window.

"Are you getting this?" Noelle asked.

Gretchen was already filming. "Got it, boss."

Noelle rang the bell, not surprised to hear it play "Have a Holly Jolly Christmas." She turned to the camera and rolled her eyes. Words were not needed.

Cynthia opened the door, not surprisingly dressed as Mrs. Claus. Noelle stepped inside. An entire Christmas village stretched out on a table covered with fake snow. The tree was bursting with handmade decorations and swirled with a garland made of popcorn and cranberries.

On top of the tree, a star flashed on and off in a kaleido-scope of colors. It was enough to send someone into an epileptic seizure.

The doorbell rang again, and when Cynthia went to answer it, Noelle turned to the camera with a grin. "Looks like Christmas exploded in here." Gretchen panned the room for added effect, then turned to the doorway where Colin stood. "And here's our guest crafter," Noelle said. "The esteemed mayor of Evergreen Creek, Colin Bennett."

Colin gave a gracious bow, waved to the camera, and walked inside.

Noelle turned to Cynthia. "So today, we're going to show our viewers a do-it-yourself craft. What will we be making today?"

Cynthia led them to a craft table supplied with green-ery, wires, and hot glue guns. "Today, we're making mistletoe ornaments. As you can see, it takes very little preparation and is easy enough for beginners."

"God help me," Noelle murmured. She followed Colin to the craft table and took a seat. She picked up the glue gun. "I've never used one of these."

"Join the club."

"There's a glue gun club?"

"No, an amateur crafting club. I'm the president."

"That's a step up from mayor."

"Does that turn you on?"

Noelle wrinkled her nose. "In your dreams."

Colin laughed. He leaned close and, in a husky whis-per, asked, "How do you know what I'm dreaming about?"

Noelle felt something shift inside her. The flirtation wasn't just for the camera anymore.

Cynthia pulled out a notebook and started reading facts about mistletoe to the camera. "Mistletoe is a symbol of love, hope, and friendship. Mistletoe is commonly used as a decoration around Christmas time. If you and someone else are under the mistletoe, you're supposed to kiss. Kissing under the mistletoe is said to bring good luck and bad luck if you don't kiss under it."

Noelle glanced at Gretchen, who shrugged. Still, she wasn't convinced Gretchen didn't have a hand in this mistletoe madness.

Cynthia took her place at the craft table. "First, we're going to cut the mistletoe into six-inch sections and secure them with a rubber band."

While Noelle and Colin followed her instructions, Cynthia continued her monologue. "If you have pets in the house, I recommend using artificial mistletoe since the berries can be poisonous to animals."

Noelle pretended to feed a berry to Colin, who played along with exaggerated shock.

Trying to maintain control, Cynthia continued her lesson. "Wrap a ribbon around the rubber band, then make a loop for hanging. Secure it with your glue gun."

Noelle couldn't get her glue gun to work, so Colin leaned over and pressed on the glue stick. That did the trick, and she ended up with a string of glue that wouldn't let go. She tried twirling it like a spaghetti strand, then reached out to pinch the glue. Everyone yelled no, but it was too late. The hot glue stuck to her fingers, and she shouted, shaking her hand. "Oww, that's hot!" She stuck her fingers in her mouth to ease the burn.

"Want me to kiss it?" Colin teased.

Without thinking, she held out her hand. At first, he looked surprised, then he brushed his lips gently over the burn on her outstretched hand. He took his time, leaving a trail of slow, soft air kisses along her fingers. Her stomach did a slow roll. Even his air kisses really did make the burn feel better.

She remembered people were watching and pulled her hand away. "Well, other than the third-degree burn, that was pretty easy," Noelle told the camera.

"We're not done," Cynthia said. She gestured to an assortment of glitter, beads, and ribbon. "Now, you can decorate your mistletoe however you like."

Noelle picked up the glitter spray. "I choose to decorate mine without using a glue gun."

"Good choice," Colin said. He picked up the glue gun and pretended to burn himself, then held out his finger with a boyish pout.

Noelle laughed. She took his hand and gave his pretend burn a few air kisses as well. "All better."

His gaze softened, and his lips parted ever so slightly. She wondered what it would be like to kiss those lips. She didn't want to think about kissing Colin, but like a song stuck in her head, that was all she could think about.

With the ornaments finished, Cynthia brought out eggnog and a platter of Christmas cookies. Noelle nibbled on a cookie. All the while, Colin stared at her lips. Noelle wondered if he was thinking the same thing she was. "Eat a cookie," she demanded with exasperation.

He gave her a naughty smile that spoke volumes, creating even more erotic thoughts. She felt heat rush to her cheeks and had to turn away. She stood and held up her mistletoe ornament, speaking to the camera. "And there you have it. Our thanks to Cynthia for inviting us into her lovely home and sponsoring our first DIY craft hour. I hope you learned something new, and I hope someone finds you under the mistletoe. This is Noelle Hamilton, signing off."

She thanked Cynthia for her hospitality, then picked up her bags and turned to go.

"Leaving so soon?" Colin asked.

She didn't want to. She wanted to be wherever Colin was, but that was a dangerous thought. "I'm going to get a head start on putting this footage together."

He leaned close enough that she could feel the heat of his breath against her neck. "Will I see you later?"

Her heart gave a little thump. "Most likely," she said. "I still have a job to do." She could read the disappointment on his face. Yeah, she had a job to do. Maybe there was more to it, but she was trying hard not to admit to herself how much she wanted to be around Colin for more personal reasons.

"Guess I'll see you around then," he said, then left.

Gretchen gave Noelle a knowing look but didn't say a word. She was quiet on the way back to the lodge. Noelle was grateful since she was lost in her own thoughts. Her feelings for Colin were confusing. It wasn't as if she hadn't had relationships before, but they were always short-term, and she called the shots. Colin felt like a long-term kind of guy, and she felt a bit out of control around him. Besides, she was leaving in a few days. She couldn't let her heart get involved. That was a lesson she'd learned a long time ago.

When they reached the lodge, Noelle asked if Gretchen wanted to come in for a drink.

"No. I think I need to go over some figures."

Noelle didn't like the sound of her voice. "Is there a problem?"

Gretchen shook her head. "Let me review the numbers, and I'll get back to you."

That didn't sound good. But Noelle had other things on her mind. She needed some time to put the finishing touches on her secret project. Time flew by, and when she heard a knock at the door, she was surprised to see that hours had passed.

Gretchen stood at the doorway, a spreadsheet in her hand. Noelle pushed aside her laptop and pulled another chair to the desk. They sat side by side with the spreadsheet on the desk between them.

"Engagement is good," Gretchen said. "But you can see here it's started to plateau."

Noelle tipped her head and stared at the spreadsheet. "I thought you said people liked the interaction between me and Colin?"

"Yes, on the live feeds. But we're losing some of our long-term subscribers. They seem disappointed."

Noelle gave her a puzzled look. "Explain."

"Your quips don't have the bite they used to. That's what people love about your videos." Gretchen frowned. "It's like you've gotten soft, especially where Colin is concerned."

At Noelle's shocked expression, Gretchen rushed on. "I get it. Colin is one hot mayor."

If that was all there was to him, Noelle wouldn't be so torn. She could ignore hot, but Colin was more than that. He was loyal to his family and friends and a hard worker with a good heart. "Yes, but he has other good traits as well."

"I agree. That's not the point."

Noelle nodded. "It's me, right? I've lost my edge." She pulled her lips together. Another reason to avoid entanglements. But... "Maybe I do have a little crush on him," she admitted.

Gretchen sat back and sighed. "I'm not surprised. He's quite a hunk. And I could see the flirting was getting hotter. But this is the first time I've seen you have real feelings for someone."

"I come off as a cold-hearted bitch?"

Gretchen smiled. "No. You're just focused, that's all. Your career has always been the most important thing in your life. I didn't think you had time for relationships."

Noelle realized Gretchen was right. She'd avoided intimate relationships and friendships because she *was* focused on her career. Gretchen was the closest thing she had to a girlfriend, but was that simply because they worked together? How many times had Gretchen suggested they go out for dinner or a drink, but Noelle had brushed her off because she had work to do? Maybe she could have friends and relationships but still keep her edge for the camera.

"You're right," she said. "I've lost my edge. This whole Christmas thing has made me soft. But I'll turn it around and give our viewers what they want."

"That should bring the ratings back up," Gretchen said with a sigh of relief. She folded the spreadsheet and put it in her pocket. "What are your plans for the day?"

"I'm running over to the marketplace. I had a little secret project that's ready to go live. I'll tell you how it works out. What about you?"

"Geoff is taking me to lunch, then we'll hang around the festival for a few hours before our meeting with Stuart at three o'clock."

"I'll be back in plenty of time," Noelle said. She wasn't looking forward to a dressing down by Stuart, especially if Gretchen's numbers were right. She'd have to find a way to bring them up again. Her job was at stake.

# Chapter Thirteen

COLIN HAD HOPED to run into Noelle at lunchtime, but she was nowhere to be found. He wondered if they would be awkward after their mutual flirtation at Cynthia's house. He hoped not.

Angela stepped into his office. "Which would you like first, the good or bad news?"

Colin blew out a breath. "I could use some good news."

"Okay, the good news is donations are up. If things keep going the way they are, we'll make our goal."

"Well, that's definitely good news. I think we can thank Noelle for the uptick in donations."

"Yes, she had a part. But don't discount all the hard work, time, and energy you've put into making the festival successful. Everyone in town pitched in as well."

"Absolutely."

Angela leaned one hip against his desk. "Speaking of Noelle. I watched some of her videos online."

Colin was surprised. Angela was technically challenged, to say the least.

"I had Davey show me how to get on YouTube."

Colin couldn't help laughing. Davey was Angela's twelve-year-old grandson. "How much did it cost you?"

"Three chocolate chip cookies and a glass of chocolate milk."

"Knowing Davey, that was a bargain."

Angela cleared her throat. "So anyway, I was watching some of Noelle's videos, and there seems to be a lot of chemistry between the two of you. I noticed that the other night at dinner as well. As your surrogate mother, I have to ask if there's something serious there."

Colin shrugged one shoulder. "She's not as bad as I first thought. She comes off as this dragon lady, but…" He stopped. What *were* his feelings toward her? It was confusing. On the one hand, he hated when she used that sarcastic tone and painted the town in a bad light. On the other hand, she was driving business to the festival, which would help them meet their goals.

And then there was the chemistry Angela had pointed out. There was no denying the way she made him feel. When was the last time a woman made him feel both vulnerable and excited at the same time?

"You didn't answer my question," Angela said. "Is there something more serious there?"

"Maybe. But she's not a townie. She'll be gone in a few days, then life will get back to normal around here." And that was the crux of the matter. Why develop a relationship with someone who was leaving in a few days?

Colin sighed. "So what's the bad news?"

"It's those darn Vonn cousins. I've been getting complaints about them all morning."

Colin shook his head. He'd had enough. "That's it. I'm about to revoke their permits and send them home."

"I'm right behind you."

They made their way to the marketplace, expecting to hear a commotion from the Vonn cousins' table. Instead, they were shocked to discover Randy and Otis were not fighting. In fact, they were downright jovial. Randy was even drinking a cup of Otis's hot chocolate. What the heck happened?

Connor stopped in front of the cousins' table. "I had reports you two were fighting again."

Randy spoke up first. "We were, but then Noelle helped us set up a website to sell our crafts online."

"It's called *It's a Vonnderful Life*," Otis said.

Yeah, that had a Noelle ring to it. Apparently, she *had* gotten something out of the movie they watched the other night.

"She even got us some publicity," Otis added.

Randy elbow-bumped his cousin. "And we've had orders come in all afternoon, haven't we?"

"Right on," Otis said. "We'll be so busy filling orders, there won't be time to fight."

"We owe it all to Noelle," Randy said with a wide-open smile. "There's no need to fight over table space when there's more than enough room in our online store to sell our crafts."

Colin was stunned. He turned to Angela. "See? Underneath that tough exterior is a heart of gold."

Angela frowned. "Depends."

"On what?"

"On whether she did it out of the goodness of her heart or if she did it just for publicity."

Colin didn't think it mattered either way. Her thoughtfulness not only made the cousins happy but solved one of Colin's problems as well. It was a win-win.

"I don't mean to be so hard on her," Angela continued. "She was delightful at dinner. It's just that there seem to be two sides to her. The sweet one I saw last night and the sarcastic one she portrays online. I can't help but wonder which is the real Noelle."

Colin nodded. "That's what I'm trying to find out."

"Good luck with that." Angela gave him a hug, then turned to leave. "I'll see you back at the office."

He watched her go, thinking about what she'd said. He'd seen the same thing. Noelle could be sweet and charming one minute, then caustic the next. He had a feeling the sarcastic Noelle was just a protective shell, but he wasn't one hundred percent sure. And with the festival halfway over, he didn't have enough time to really find out.

While he was at the marketplace, he decided to check in with the vendors. The consensus was that they were all doing much better than last year. Mrs. Claus, who was actually Priscilla from the library, had completely sold out of her boozy cakes. A sign on her station said, "Going back to the North Pole to make more cakes. Be back this afternoon. Leave your name and phone number for special requests." The sign-up sheet was half-filled. It looked like Priscilla would be up all night baking.

Beverly Flynn's table was filled with her handmade pottery. Beverly owned the Pottery Club in town, where people came for lessons and to have their clay pottery fired. She was an excellent teacher and an artist in her own right. Many of her items could be purchased online, and from what he heard, she was doing very well.

Colin held up a pendant with a glossy glaze. "How do you get such vibrant colors?" he asked.

"I use mason stains to color the clay. I'm always surprised at how they come out of the kiln. Each one is unique."

Colin reached for a blue teacup decorated with dragonflies. "I was looking for a Christmas gift for Angela. This is perfect. She loves dragonflies."

"Then she'll love this. Would you like me to wrap it up for you?"

"I'd appreciate it," he said, reaching for his wallet. He looked around the table. In the back of his mind was the thought of getting something for Noelle. But it seemed presumptuous. They really didn't know each other that well. Maybe he could get her something as a thank-you gift for covering the festival. Something that wasn't too personal. But nothing seemed to fit the bill.

In the end, he paid for his purchase and left.

On his way out, he saw a tray of ceramic ornaments. Maybe an ornament wasn't too personal. She must at least have a Christmas tree in her apartment. He looked through them and picked out a few for gifts — an ornament shaped like a stack of books for Priscilla, a baby wearing a Santa hat for Kelly, and a stained-glass dragonfly ornament for Angela. He was about to leave when he spotted another ornament. Considering he hoped she'd join him at the ice skating rink later this evening, the porcelain skates ornament could be the perfect gift for Noelle. Not too personal, but meaningful. At least, he hoped so.

# Chapter Fourteen

BACK AT THE LODGE, Noelle and Gretchen were in the middle of a video chat with Stuart, who had a permanent frown on his face. "I've noticed your numbers are slipping again," he said. "How can you mess up Christmas?"

"It's hard to make fun of Santa Claus," Noelle quipped. "You'll end up on his naughty list."

"That's not the list you should be worried about," Stuart shot back.

Gretchen spoke up. "I've done some deep research, and it seems like the dip is more of a transition. Yes, we're losing the subscribers who only came here to watch Noelle decimate someone, but the new subscribers are in love with Noelle's softer side. They tune in specifically to watch her interaction with Colin. They're vocal and loyal and bring a fresh perspective to the channel."

Stuart gave her a thoughtful look. "So you're saying the subscribers we're losing weren't as active as the ones we're gaining?"

"Basically, yes."

Noelle glanced at Gretchen. Was that true, or was she

sugarcoating it for Stuart's sake? Either way, she was grateful and determined to do her own investigating once the call was over.

Stuart took a deep breath. "Well, let's see if that's the case. Finish out the rest of the festival, and we'll decide where to go from there."

Stuart signed off without a goodbye. Noelle and Gretchen stared at each other. Gretchen shrugged, and Noelle rolled her eyes.

"So," Noelle said. "Which direction should I go? Naughty or nice?"

Gretchen pretended to think about it. "My advice? Go with your heart. The more real you are, the more the viewers will respond either way."

That, Noelle thought, was the best advice anyone could give.

After Gretchen left, Noelle dug into the analytics and found that Gretchen had nailed it. They weren't getting the number of views they were accustomed to, but the new subscribers were far more engaged than the ones who dropped. Was that enough, though? She wasn't going to force an attraction to Colin just to appeal to viewers. On the other hand, the chemistry was definitely there, and if Gretchen was right, she'd lost her edge because of it.

When someone knocked on the door, she assumed it was Gretchen. To her surprise, Colin stood there, as if she'd conjured him with her thoughts. He seemed bigger, filling the doorway. She was suddenly aware that they were alone together in her room.

"I thought you could use a break," he said. "A little birdie told me you've been slaving away at the books all afternoon."

"Is that little birdie named Gretchen?"

He nodded. "I ran into Gretchen and Geoff a little

while ago. They were having an early dinner, and I realized you probably hadn't eaten." He gave her a shy smile. "I still owe you dinner for helping me with the sausage truck the other day."

She was about to decline, but just then, her stomach rumbled, and she knew she wouldn't get away with saying she wasn't hungry. "On one condition," she said.

"That is?"

"No sausage and peppers."

He let loose with a rumbling laugh. "I have a condition as well," he said.

"Which is?"

"No cameras."

"Agreed." At least that way, she didn't have to worry about how she should act for the viewers. She could just be herself.

"I was hoping you'd agree. I made reservations for the two of us at a nearby steakhouse."

"Oh." A steakhouse? That felt more like a date than grabbing a slice of pizza at the festival. She suddenly felt shy and a bit nervous. She looked down at what she was wearing — black slacks and a burgundy sweater over a black t-shirt. "I'm not dressed for dinner at a steakhouse."

"You look great," he said. "It's very casual."

She could almost feel the heat of his gaze. He added, "Besides, you don't want to be overdressed since we're going ice skating afterward."

"Oh, I don't skate."

"Then now's a good time to learn." He reached out and took her hand. "I'll be right beside you."

That wasn't the problem. There was a reason she didn't want to go ice skating. But she'd save that conversation for later. No sense spoiling dinner. She grabbed her coat and followed Colin to his car.

The restaurant was quaint, decorated with dark paneling and warm candlelight. The air smelled of wood fire and roasted meat, making her taste buds sing. They sat at an intimate corner booth. Colin was greeted by the owner, who sent over a bottle of wine "on the house."

Colin filled their glasses and raised his in a toast. "To a successful festival."

They clinked glasses. Noelle appreciated that he didn't get all boujee by sniffing the cork and pretending he could tell what notes were in the wine or how long it was aged in an oak barrel. He just drank it and gave a low moan of appreciation that rippled down Noelle's spine.

She tried not to think about what that might sound like in the bedroom and made a show of looking over the menu. "What would you recommend?"

"Their prime rib is tender and perfectly seasoned. If you don't want beef, I'd recommend the chicken marsala or a classic Cobb salad."

Noelle opted for the chicken. She sipped on her wine. It had a light flavor, not too dry and not too sweet.

After they ordered, Colin turned to her and asked why she hated Christmas.

Noelle nearly choked on her wine. "I don't hate Christmas."

"It seems that way."

"I just don't go all slobbery over Christmas and stuff."

Colin gave her a long, hard stare. Long enough that Noelle started getting nervous as if he could see right through her. She squirmed in her chair. "Okay. Maybe I have some feelings about the holiday. It's not my favorite, okay?"

She wasn't one to talk about her past, but it was getting harder and harder not to share her feelings with Colin. Maybe if he knew why it was such a difficult holiday for her, he'd be more understanding. She wasn't cold-hearted. She just had issues. Everyone had issues, right?

"Shouldn't you be at the festival?" she asked.

He grinned, obviously aware of her awkward attempt to change the subject. "Everything's covered for the next few hours. We'll have time to go ice skating."

"Yeah, about that…"

"I won't take no for an answer."

Noelle opened her mouth, then closed it again. Just then, the server arrived with their meals, so she was saved from having to respond. Colin was right. The meal was delicious, tender, and fragrant. Everything was cooked to perfection, and they finished the wine while avoiding any conversation too deep or personal.

At one point, Colin reached for her hand. "Look," he said, lifting his chin and gesturing toward the window. A light, feathery snow drifted down.

"Oh, that's pretty." It really was. She had nothing against snow. At least when it fell like a picture postcard. Blizzards filled with stinging ice pellets weren't fun, and muddy slush would never grace a Norman Rockwell print. But this light and airy snow was delightful to look at.

Maybe she was going soft. The old Noelle would have said something biting about the slush, ice, and dangerous sidewalks as if the snow itself was nothing but a hazard.

Colin squeezed her hand and smiled. "Kinda puts you in the Christmas spirit, doesn't it?"

Surprisingly, it did. She nodded. Yeah, she was definitely growing soft.

"Will you be spending Christmas with your family?" he asked.

Noelle shook her head. "Nope. My parents are divorced. They live on opposite ends of the country, as far away from each other as possible. My mother is in Port-land, Oregon, and my father is in Tampa, Florida."

"Sisters? Brothers?"

"Nope. I'm an only child. Apparently, I was such a disappointment they decided not to have any more children."

Colin squeezed her hand. "I doubt that was the case."

Noelle started to make a smart comment, then stopped herself. She was so used to cracking a joke to hide the deep hurt inside that it came automatically. Colin saw right through her.

"You're right. They probably shouldn't have gotten married in the first place. It was a shotgun wedding because my mother was pregnant with me." She lowered her voice. "They fought all the time. That's all I remember."

She'd always thought the divorce was her fault. Even now, she carried the blame for it, as if being a child was enough to destroy a marriage. She knew that wasn't the case, but the little girl in her still believed they didn't love her enough to stay together.

"You, on the other hand," she said, "seem to have had the perfect childhood."

"Far from perfect," he replied. "But yes, I'm one of the lucky ones. An only child like you, but my parents made sure I had what I needed while still instilling a sense of responsibility in me."

"Your dad?"

"Pancreatic cancer," he said, answering her unspoken question. "Then Mom followed soon after." He choked back a sob. "Suddenly, I was an adult orphan." He blinked back tears. "Luckily, Angela stepped in to fill some of that emptiness. She knows she can't take my mother's place, but she does a hell of a job trying."

Noelle reached across the table for Colin's hand and squeezed it. "I can see she adores you."

His eyes glistened. "The feeling is mutual."

Just then, the server came by to clear their plates. "I have a special surprise," he said. "We're introducing a special holiday dessert, and you'll be the first to try it." He stepped aside, and Noelle watched in awe as another server arrived with what looked like a Christmas tree on a silver platter. He set it on the table, then lit the sparkler on top, which sparkled and glittered.

Their server placed two spoons on the table and then explained. "This is made with an upside-down ice cream cone on top of a brownie base. The cone is then decorated with whipped cream mixed with green food coloring and drizzled with hot fudge and sprinkles. The sparkler represents the star at the top of the tree. If you make a wish and it comes true, the next meal is on us."

The sparkler sizzled out. "Oops, too late," the server said with a smile.

"You planned that, didn't you?"

"Maybe. It's kind of fun, though, isn't it?"

Colin grinned. "Yeah, it's impressive. However, I'd leave out the part about making a wish then snatching it away."

"So…?" He waited for them to try it.

Noelle went first, digging into the brownie and ice cream at the base. "Mmm…delicious!"

Colin first pulled the sparkler out of the top. "Choking hazard," he said. Then he buried his spoon into the sugar cone. "Oh, yeah. This one's a keeper."

Noelle reached over and wiped a bit of ice cream from the side of his mouth. Their gazes held for a long moment. He held the sparkler out. "Make a wish."

"It doesn't work if the sparkler is burned out."

"Oh, you're the authority on sparklers now?"

"No, I'm the authority on wishes." She'd made enough of them, and none had ever come true.

"Close your eyes," he said.

She closed her eyes.

"Now, see the sparkler in your mind. Glowing and sparkling and making all those sparkling sounds."

She opened one eye and smiled. "Sparkling sounds?"

"Shush. Eyes closed. Now, can you see it?"

She nodded.

"Then blow it out and make a wish."

She took a deep breath. In her mind, she saw the sparkler flare up, then extinguish when she blew on it. She made the first wish that came to her mind. She wished she deserved a man like Colin and all he represented. But, like all her wishes, she knew this one would never come true.

# Chapter Fifteen

AFTER DINNER, Colin and Noelle walked to the skating rink. Ice skaters glided across the ice, scarves flowing behind them. Noelle was surprised at how many people were gathered there, some skating and others drinking hot cider around a campfire. A light dusting of snow covered the pine trees in the background. With the flakes falling, the scene reminded her of her most treasured possession, the snow globe her grandfather had given her when she was twelve. Her vision blurred as tears filled her eyes.

Colin wrapped an arm around her. "Hey, are you okay?"

Maybe it was the wine, or missing her grandfather, or the comfort of Colin's embrace, but she cracked. Tears flowed, and when she sniffled, Colin handed her a clean and perfectly folded handkerchief. That gesture was the final nudge to push her over the edge, and she broke down in sobs.

Colin led her toward a bench. He took off his jacket and placed it on the bench seat, then urged her to sit. He moved in close beside her. The heat of his body surrounded her, and she breathed in the smell she'd come to recognize as his, a combination of pine and sage. She leaned into him as tears she'd held in for years finally found release.

He rubbed her back, not pushing her to explain. Simply being there. And for that, she owed him an explanation. Once the tears stopped and she could speak without sobbing, she sat back and gave him a grateful nod.

"If I'd known it would upset you," Colin said. "I wouldn't have asked you to skate."

She laughed, sliding from one emotion to the next. She took a deep breath and looked out over the pond at the children skating, with snow falling softly around them. "It's so beautiful," she said. "It reminds me of a snow globe my grandfather gave me when I was young."

"And that made you cry?"

She leaned her head on his shoulder. "Yes. And no. The snow globe reminded me why Christmas was so hard for me. When I was eight, all I wanted for Christmas was a pair of skates. I'd written letters to Santa and circled the skates I wanted from an advertisement. All I talked about was getting my own pair of skates and going ice skating down at the park."

Colin waited patiently, allowing her to explore her memories and bring them out of the dark. "As the weeks led up to Christmas, the tree remained bare, the house undecorated. My parents fought night and day."

He rubbed her arm, silently urging her to talk.

"Christmas morning, there was nothing under the tree. No skates, no stockings, no Christmas cookies. My father was nowhere to be seen, and my mother snatched me up, still in my pajamas, and bundled me in the car. We were on the road for days."

The memory still filled her with guilt.

*"Do you think Santa forgot my ice skates, Mom?"*

*Her mother's face twisted with anger. "Will you shut up about those damn skates? We have more important things to worry about."*

That was true then and for years later, as her mother struggled to provide for them both. They ended up as far away from everything she considered home as possible. Her parents divorced, and there was no Christmas that year. Or the year after. And for some reason, she blamed herself. Maybe if she hadn't asked for skates, her parents could have concentrated on their marriage and not gotten a divorce. She knew that wasn't the case as an adult, but the child inside still blamed herself.

Noelle glanced up at Colin. "And then, one day, my mother left me on my grandfather's doorstep. She said she had a job out of state and didn't want to uproot me again. That may or may not have been the truth. She says I begged to stay with him. Maybe it was a combination of both."

Noelle took a deep breath and let it out with a sigh. "But honestly, she did me a favor. My grandfather was the most stable relationship I'd known."

"And he's the one who gave you the ice-skating snow globe."

Noelle nodded. "I loved the snow globe, but it was bittersweet. I knew I'd never ask for ice skates again or skate around an iced-over pond with my friends."

"Your grandfather?"

"He passed away a few years ago."

"So you're all alone?"

She shook her head. "No. I have Gretchen. And my parents each send me a Christmas card every year."

He didn't say a word. She could feel his heartbeat against her cheek. All these years, she'd blamed herself, assuming that simply asking for something led to abandonment. As if she didn't deserve to be loved. Maybe she'd avoided relationships for that reason.

Colin pulled her close, and she didn't resist. "No wonder you hate Christmas."

"I don't hate Christmas."

"I know, you just don't get all googly-eyed about it."

She smiled, and time seemed to stand still. He gazed at her lips, and she tipped her head back.

But just then, a cheer went up from the crowd. People were looking up and pointing. And there, in the sky, for the first time in her life, Noelle saw the northern lights putting on a dazzling display of pinks, purples, reds, and greens. It seemed like a sign.

"I had no idea you could see the northern lights from here," she said.

"It's rare, but it does happen."

"I'm glad I got to see it." With you, she added but didn't say out loud. Somehow, the pulsating light display showing up at this moment with this man beside her felt like a sign.

Colin gripped her hand as they enjoyed the rare light show together. She felt comfortable, warm, and protected in Colin's embrace. And lighter somehow, as if purging herself of guilt and abandonment had lifted a weight from her heart.

"I was thinking," Colin said, still staring up at the sky. "I'm no psychologist, but is it possible the reason you avoid Christmas is that you're punishing yourself over your imagined part in your parents' divorce?"

Noelle thought about it. The way Colin phrased the question made sense. She hadn't thought about it in quite that way before. "It's possible," she said.

He lowered his gaze and smiled. "Then there's no reason to be a Grinch anymore."

She chuckled. "We'll see."

"Baby steps," he said. "And I think the first step might be putting on a pair of skates."

She shook her head vehemently. "No, I couldn't."

He gave her a long, lingering look. "Why not? You're not that young girl anymore. You're an adult who can make grown-up decisions. Besides, we're only putting them on, that's all." He pursed his lips. "As Angela would say, you have to get back on the horse."

"You have a horse?"

"It's a metaphor."

"I know." She quietly considered it. Why not?

"What size shoes do you wear?" he asked.

"Seven and a half," she replied, all but admitting she was willing to go along with his baby steps theory.

"I'll be right back."

While he was gone, Noelle watched the skaters filled with both trepidation and longing. Could something as simple as putting on a pair of ice skates start to heal the wounds inside? She thought of her grandfather's snow globe. It was as if she was seeing it come to life all around her.

And because memories of her grandfather gave her the courage she needed, when Colin came back with the skates, she eagerly put them on. She wobbled when she stood, but only for a moment. It really wasn't that much different from rollerblading, which she'd done for years.

Colin put his arm around her shoulders to steady her. "Ready?" he asked.

She gave him a tentative nod. They crunched through the snow to the pond. She stepped onto the ice, then gently shoved off, hesitant at first, then gaining confidence as Colin stayed by her side. They skated together, arm in arm. The air was crisp, and the wind rustled through her hair as she glided across the ice. She felt free as if a weight had been lifted from her shoulders. Why had she waited so long to overcome her fear? Why had she let it grow bigger and bigger until it was an insurmountable obstacle?

She turned to Colin. "Thank you," she said. With that, she let go of his arm and skated away. Colin cheered her on. She hadn't felt so light and free in years. And she owed it all to Colin and his metaphorical horse.

# Chapter Sixteen

Once she started skating, Noelle didn't want to stop. Colin took her arm. "That's enough, tiger."

"But…"

"No buts. Your thighs will thank me in the morning."

She slowed to a stop and smiled a smile of pure happiness. "I did it," she whispered.

"You did. And I'm proud of you."

They sat on the bench and took off their skates. As the air cooled, Noelle started to shiver. "What's next on the agenda? Someplace warm, I hope."

"As a matter of fact, I'm the guest caller for bingo in half an hour. Want to join me?"

She rolled her eyes. "Can I film it?"

"Yeah, but I have to warn you. Those bingo players can get pretty rowdy."

"I'll take my chances."

They stopped for hot chocolate on their way to take the chill off. Noelle took the opportunity to call Gretchen and ask her to bring the camera to the bingo event at the community hall. They walked to the community hall arm in arm. The air was crisp and fresh. A light dusting of snow made everything look like life-sized Christmas ornaments. "Your town is very pretty," she admitted.

"Thank you. I'm sure it's not as exciting as living in the big city."

"No, but there's a certain charm about a small town. Knowing your neighbors and everyone's routines."

"I wouldn't live anywhere else."

Noelle wondered if she could give up the energy and excitement of New York City to live in a small town. Both had their pros and cons. But the small town had something the city didn't have. It had Colin.

Tables were set up in the community hall, and people filed in, filling the room quickly. "I had no idea bingo was so popular," Noelle said.

"Oh, just wait and see. We had to cancel during the pandemic, and people went nuts. It was one of the first things we brought back when quarantine ended."

As they passed a row of tables, Noelle was surprised to see people with more cards than she would have thought possible to keep up with. Some decorated their spots with little troll dolls and good-luck charms. She realized something immediately, however. Everyone was visiting other tables, laughing, and socializing. Maybe they were serious about their bingo, but more than that, it was a way for the community to get together. A few weeks ago, she would have hated the thought of a group communal event to exchange pleasantries with neighbors, but somehow, now it all made sense in what she was learning about small-town life.

They made their way to the stage, where a cageful of balls bounced around like popcorn in a hot pan. Colin checked the microphone, and the crowd shouted greetings. "Are we ready to bingo?" he shouted.

The crowd cheered.

"I'll be your caller tonight. And we also have a guest caller helping me."

Noelle leaned into the microphone. "Because reading numbers is hard," she quipped. She was surprised by a burst of laughter from the crowd.

"My helper tonight is the slightly acerbic but lovely Noelle Hamilton from Your Social Media Source. I'm sure most of you have seen her around town, inter- viewing our local celebrities and documenting the festival."

A smattering of applause. Noelle got the impression some of these people had seen her videos and weren't impressed. For some reason, that made her want to change their opinion. Weird. When was the last time she cared whether anyone liked her or not?

Colin called the first number. "I-29."

Noelle leaned into the microphone. "No, he's not."

A smattering of chuckles from the crowd.

"Don't encourage her," Colin said.

He called a few more numbers until someone yelled, "Shake 'em up." He glanced at Noelle, who shrugged her shoulders. She had no idea how to shake them up, either. Their gazes held for a long moment and only broke off when someone in the crowd yelled for them to get on with it.

Colin resumed calling. "G-51."

"Are we having fun?"

The crowd cheered.

When he called O-69, Noelle smacked her lips and then made a locking motion in front of her mouth. Colin glanced over and rolled his eyes, pretending exasperation, but the crowd loved it.

By the time they were done and several winners had

collected their prizes, Noelle could tell the crowd was on her side.

"They loved you," Colin said.

For some crazy reason, that filled her with satisfaction. "And you?"

He grinned. "You're growing on me."

"Like mold, huh?"

Colin's face grew serious. "Do you always do that?"

"Do what?"

"Make a joke when things get too serious?"

"I joke all the time, serious or not."

He waited a moment, then shrugged. "Okay."

But it didn't sound okay. It sounded like he was letting her off the hook for now.

Colin walked her back to the lodge, which was only a few blocks away. "How would you like to go snowmobiling with me tomorrow?"

"Depends. Are you going to break down and leave us stranded again?"

"I'll try not to. But if there's anyone I'd rather be stranded with, it would be you."

That simple statement sent butterflies to her stomach and a smile to her face.

"How does ten sound?" he asked.

"I'll be ready," she said, then went inside, already looking forward to the next day.

A long, hot bath felt good after coming in from the cold. She lit a candle and luxuriated in the fragrant bubbles. She was usually too busy to enjoy a bath, choosing instead to pop in and out of the shower, but tonight felt different. It felt like a night to relax and pamper herself.

She heard her text message beep, but she'd left her phone in the other room and chose to ignore it. There wasn't anything that couldn't wait another ten minutes or so. She wouldn't have thought that a few months ago when she spent her days like a hamster on a running wheel, but something about this sleepy little town had her slowing down the pace.

When she came out of the bathroom, she checked her phone. There was a text from Colin. *Sweet dreams* was all it said, but those two words brought a lump to her throat.

Relaxed after her bath, she curled up on a chair and wrapped the blanket from the bed around herself. She downloaded a book she'd been hearing about and read until her eyes grew tired. Then she slept more soundly than she'd slept in months.

As USUAL, Colin picked her up at precisely ten the following day. Noelle put on the extra helmet he'd brought and climbed on the back of the sled right behind him. She put her arms around his waist and leaned into his back as he took off with a roar.

Colin dipped and spun the sled through snow-covered fields. The speed was exhilarating, and the crisp air turned her cheeks red. Other than the tracks from their snowmobile, the snow was unblemished — white, clean, and pure. At one point, he sped up and bounced over a small hill, lifting them both off the seat. Her stomach dropped, and she found herself laughing out loud.

To Noelle's surprise, they ended up at the cabin, only this time the windows were all lit up. A freshly cut pine tree was inside, and Christmas carols played softly in the background. A few presents were hastily wrapped and placed beneath the tree alongside boxes of ornaments and tinsel.

Colin looked anxious. "Your story touched me. It made me realize how much I'd taken for granted growing up.

Christmas was a time to celebrate and spend time with family and friends. I wanted to, I don't know … make up for the Christmases you lost. I wanted to make Christmas something you could look forward to and erase all those bad memories."

Noelle felt a tightening in her chest. She blinked back tears. "That's…" Her voice caught on a sob. "That's sweet."

"If you don't want to…"

"No. It's okay." She wasn't exactly sure how she felt. On the one hand, it was the sweetest thing anyone had ever done for her. But on the other hand, it brought back feelings of inadequacy. For just a moment, she was a young girl wondering why no one loved her enough to give her that storybook Christmas everyone else enjoyed. Even Santa Claus had let her down.

But not Colin. He'd gone out of his way to give her this one special Christmas to make up for the ones she'd lost along the way. She pinched a pine needle and lifted it to her nose. The aroma of pine held every Christmas wish she'd ever made.

She glanced at the boxes under the tree. "Are these for me?"

"Yes, but not until after we decorate the tree. It's a Christmas tradition." He pushed forward a box filled with ornaments. "These are ornaments my family has gathered over the years. Some were purchased for a special occasion." He held up an ornament of a small boy holding a baseball bat. "This was when my Little League team won the championship."

Noelle took it from his hand and placed it on a pine branch.

"And this one," he said, holding up a small crystal angel, "this was on my grandmother's tree. We inherited it when she passed." He smiled and placed it high on the tree.

Noelle pulled out a blue ornament. "Cookie Monster?"

Colin grinned. "When I was little, all I wanted was cookies. My mother and Angela started calling me their little cookie monster.

"Ah. Angela still does," Noelle said, remembering the other night at her house.

Colin smiled and nodded. "One year, my mother baked a cake shaped like Cookie Monster for my birthday. That year, I received all Cookie Monster gifts — toys, t-shirts, pajamas, and Legos."

Noelle smiled at the story and the image of him as a young boy surrounded by Cookie Monster toys.

"I was in heaven," he admitted. "It became a running gag between the three of us. Angela continued the tradition. Every year, I get something related to Cookie Monster. Last year, it was this ornament." He pressed a button, and the ornament lit up. A familiar voice growled, "Me want cookie!" Colin smiled and placed it lovingly on the tree.

"Every year?"

"Yep. It may seem silly, but most traditions start out like that … a random comment, a love of cookies, a favorite topper on the Christmas tree. After my parents passed away, Angela was the one who worked to keep those traditions alive."

"And so every year, you make sure she has a tree and Christmas gifts beneath it."

"Yeah."

Noelle's heart melted. She turned away to hide the tears that stung her eyes.

They continued decorating the tree together. Each

ornament had a story that went with it. Between the two of them, they decorated the entire tree.

"It looks great," Noelle said.

"Not done yet." Colin tore open a package of silver tinsel. "There's a method to placing tinsel on the tree," he said. He pulled out three or four strands and combed them downward, letting them drip like real icicles. "My mother was very meticulous about it."

"So," she said with a grin, "she wouldn't have liked this?" She took a handful of tinsel and threw it on the tree with utter abandon.

"Noooo!" he cried out in feigned shock. Then he tossed a handful over her head. Before long, they were in the middle of a tinsel fight. When it was all over, there was more tinsel on them than on the tree.

Noelle couldn't help eyeing the gifts under the tree. It amazed her how much she yearned to open those gifts as if they really could make up for the ones she hadn't received all those years ago. She was almost afraid to want it too much, only to be disappointed.

Colin leaned down and picked up one of the gifts. "I didn't have much time to shop," he said. "But I tried to find things that would remind you of us. I mean Evergreen Creek. And your time here." Color rushed to his cheeks. "And yes. Us."

She took the gift and tore the paper off, giddy as a young girl. "Oh." It was a book by Niles Nash. There was a bookmark inside, and when she turned to the marked pages, she found the poem. She read it quietly, "They searched for azure all their lives ..."

"And found it in the bluest skies," Colin finished. He held her gaze for a long, thoughtful moment that spoke volumes.

She clutched the book to her chest but didn't trust

herself to speak. The rest of the gifts were small but memorable and made her smile — a bingo game, a wind-up snowmobile, a box of hot chocolate mix from the grocery store.

"I told you I was rushed for time," he said.

"It's perfect. It's all perfect."

Every box she opened reminded her of something they'd done together or a segment she'd filmed. Then Colin handed her the final box. "This is your first orna-ment for the tree."

She opened the box to find a beautiful porcelain orna-ment in the shape of silver and white ice skates tied with red velvet laces. And this time, she couldn't stop the tears from falling. She rushed into his arms. "Thank you. This means … you don't know, it means so much to me."

"I picked these up before you told me about your aver-sion to ice skating. I had planned for us to go ice skating that evening and thought it would make a nice memory."

"It was more meaningful than you could have imag-ined," she said, tracing the outline of the skates. *Her* skates.

Colin's voice softened. "Maybe it was just meant to be." He patted her back. "Now, find a special spot to put it on the tree."

She turned and placed the ornament right at eye level so she could see it every time she looked at the tree. While she was doing that, Colin hit a switch, and the tree came to life with twinkling multi-colored lights. She caught her breath, and a delight shivered down her body. "It's perfect," she whispered. "Just perfect."

"I thought maybe if you didn't have any plans, you'd like to spend Christmas here."

There was such sincere yearning on his face that Noelle could barely look at him. "Here? At the cabin? With you?"

He nodded.

She couldn't give him a yes. Not yet. Although she was leaning in that direction. His thoughtfulness had touched her in ways she hadn't known before. "We'll see," she said.

That answer was enough for him. "At least you didn't say no."

She reached out and clasped his hand. "Thank you for this day. And thank you for the invitation."

"There's plenty of time to think about it," he suggested. "We still have a few more days before Christmas."

"And a lot more festival to cover." Although, to be honest, Noelle hadn't given much thought to covering the rest of the festival. She was having too much fun rediscovering the joy of Christmas. How had she come this far in a few short days?

"I have another surprise," Colin said, leading her into the kitchen. He went to the counter and uncovered a machine.

Noelle's eyes widened. "Is that…?"

"I had Katie at the cafe help me pick it out."

Noelle nearly swooned. It was a high-end luxury coffee machine. "Do you know how to work this?"

"Yep. Katie gave me specific instructions. Would you like an espresso?"

"I would *love* an espresso."

"Great! Why don't you get the milk and butter from the fridge while I prepare the coffee."

Noelle gave him a quizzical look. "Butter?" Maybe Katie hadn't schooled him property.

Colin started the coffee brewing, then reached into the bread box. "Cranberry nut coffee cake, fresh from Mrs. Claus's marketplace."

"How dangerous is it?" she asked, remembering the boozy fruitcake she'd sampled at Mrs. Claus's booth.

"I specifically asked for the non-alcoholic version. She looked at me like I was crazy, but I didn't want to be accused of liquoring you up to gain favor."

"With me or my video?"

"Maybe both." His slow, sexy smile made her heart melt. To cover the blush she felt rising to her cheeks, she sliced the cranberry nut bread while Colin frothed milk for the espresso. It all felt so domestic, and that was something else she wasn't accustomed to.

The coffee was aromatic, and the nut bread was sweet and buttery. Colin's thoughtfulness touched her. For the next few hours, the thought of ratings or subscribers never even entered her mind. It was hard not to relax with a cup of aromatic espresso, a roaring fire in the fireplace, and a picture-perfect Christmas tree perfectly decorated. Not to mention a hot mayor by her side.

# Chapter Seventeen

MEANWHILE, Gretchen was nursing a headache. She'd reviewed the numbers all afternoon, and it wasn't looking good. When Geoff texted asking if she'd like to go to Blitzen's for a drink, she jumped at the chance.

She turned off her computer, changed into a sparkly Christmas sweater, and went to meet Geoff at the local watering hole. They both arrived at the same time and sat at the bar.

"You look stressed," Geoff said.

"Totally. I keep crunching the numbers. We're losing subscribers, and our ratings are dropping. The way things are going, we won't have a job when we go back home."

While Noelle's segments with Colin initially drove engagement up, now it was falling, and their boss was not happy about it. She didn't let on to Geoff exactly how bad things were getting.

Their drinks came. Geoff asked, "What can we do to change that?"

Gretchen pulled the little umbrella out of her drink, took a sip, then shrugged. She liked that Geoff said *we* as if he was committed to their success as well. "I thought when the dynamics between Colin and Noelle began to shift, we were gaining a new set of viewers. But it's not enough to make up for the subscribers we've lost."

Geoff frowned. "I watched some of those videos, and it seemed like some of that chemistry was a bit forced."

"Yeah, my fault. I told Noelle to turn it on for the new subscribers."

"Well, maybe her popularity wasn't so much based on her sarcasm, but her honesty. Maybe the people who left could tell she wasn't being sincere."

Gretchen smiled at him. "I think maybe you've hit on it. It doesn't matter if she's snarky or flirty, as long as it's a real, honest reaction."

"That's the key."

Gretchen's shoulders dropped as if a weight had been lifted. "Thanks. I feel a lot better now."

"Good, that means you can relax and enjoy yourself." He lifted his drink for a toast, and they clinked glasses. "Here's to a successful fundraising festival," he said.

"And here's to still having a job when I get home," Gretchen added.

"So, I'm still working on ideas for my ice sculpture," Geoff said. "Colin wants something more traditional, but Noelle told me to go with my gut. I have some great ideas but haven't nailed them down yet."

"Need help? I'm pretty good at brainstorming."

"No. I've narrowed it down to three. It's just a matter of deciding which one to choose."

Gretchen lifted her empty glass, gesturing to the bartender for another. "Can I have a clue?"

"Nope. I want to surprise you."

God, he was adorable. She hoped Noelle hadn't given him bad advice. She wasn't sure how unconventional

Geoff might go, and he still had to live here after they left.

A woman sidled up to the bar beside Geoff. Gretchen recognized her. Anne? Annette?

She leaned over and put out her hand. "Angela," she said. "Angela Cooper."

Yeah, that was it. "I'm Gretchen. We met the other night."

"That's right." She turned to Geoff. "How is that sculpture coming along?"

"I'll know better tomorrow," he said.

The bartender came over. "The usual?" he asked Angela.

She nodded. "Add a side of tater tots."

"You got it." The bartender turned and walked away.

Angela turned to Gretchen. "Where's Noelle tonight?"

Gretchen shrugged. "I haven't seen her all afternoon. I'm assuming she's with Colin."

Angela smiled. "I hope so. I've known Colin since he was a little boy, and I've never seen him this happy. At first, I was wary of her intentions, but I think she's good for him."

Gretchen felt the same way but worried that it wouldn't end well. It was obvious Noelle was much happier than she'd ever seen her. But they'd be leaving once the festival was over.

"He's been focused solely on work ever since his mother died," Angela continued. "He thinks he has to do everything. It's nice to see him enjoying himself and delegating jobs to others."

Geoff's head bobbed up and down. "I noticed that too. He put me in charge of getting the coloring books and crayons for Santa to give the kids. I even picked up the candy canes."

Angela gave him a motherly pat on the shoulder. "I'm sure you did a great job."

Geoff glowed under her praise.

Just then, Noelle and Colin walked in. They were laughing and walking so close together that you couldn't fit a snowflake between them. It took a minute or two for them to notice the others at the bar. Colin reached out and hugged Angela, leaving his arm draped around her while Geoff told him about all the supplies he'd picked up. "Thanks, Geoff. I appreciate you stepping up."

But even while he was talking to Angela and Geoff, his gaze kept coming back to Noelle. For her part, she was catching up with Gretchen while trying not to look like someone who was smitten.

"What have you two been up to?" Gretchen asked.

Noelle glanced at Colin, then lowered her gaze with a soft smile. "We decorated a tree."

Gretchen raised an eyebrow. "Like ... a Christmas tree?"

Noelle nodded her head as if even she couldn't believe it. "Yeah. A Christmas tree. And it didn't feel corny or anything."

Gretchen couldn't believe what she was hearing. Noelle had avoided anything having to do with Christmas for as long as Gretchen had known her. Maybe all her newfound Christmas spirit wasn't an act after all.

"Well," Angela said. "I have some good news."

All eyes turned to her.

"As treasurer, I'm happy to report that we're right on track with our fundraising." She glanced at Noelle. "There's no question your channel is helping us reach our goals. If things continue at the pace we're experiencing, there's a good chance we'll raise enough not only to replace the school roof but also to repair the water damage at the library."

The group raised a cheer. Even the bartender joined in.

Angela turned to Colin. "Your mother would be proud," she said.

His eyes misted over. "Yeah, she would." He turned to Noelle. "But I couldn't have done it without Noelle and Gretchen's help."

Gretchen felt good about her part in helping the community, but she couldn't help wondering what the fallout might be if they didn't bring their ratings up.

"What's on the agenda for this afternoon?" Gretchen asked.

Colin rubbed his chin thoughtfully. "Holiday Putt-Putt, coloring pages for kids in the Community Hall, and the Reindeer Ring Toss."

"Real reindeer?" Gretchen asked, her eyes wide.

"Nope. Bowling pins painted to look like reindeer."

Gretchen's shoulders slumped. "I'm not leaving without seeing an actual reindeer."

Colin grinned. "You may be here a while." He turned to Angela. "If you cover the coloring page room, Gretchen and Geoff can run the Reindeer Ring Toss, and Noelle and I will be in charge of the Holiday Putt-Putt."

Geoff gave a mock salute. "We're on it, Mayor."

"Okay, everyone. Man your stations."

The group went to the festival grounds, then split up and went their separate ways. Noelle and Colin headed to the makeshift miniature golf course. Like everything else, it was well crafted, with snow-covered embankments and Christmas-themed obstacles. The final ball had to go directly into Rudolph's red nose.

They ran through the course first to make sure there

were no snags. Everything went smoothly, and if they'd been keeping score, it would have been close. Not that Noelle was competitive or anything.

"So, how do we score?" she asked.

"We don't score."

"Then how do we know who the winner is?"

Colin grinned. "Everyone who finishes gets a prize."

Noel frowned. "Then what's the point?"

"The point is to have fun." He pointed to a box wrapped to look like a present. "In here are baggies filled with candy canes, holiday stickers, and granola bars for the kids." He handed her an envelope. "And here are coupons donated from local businesses for the adults. Everyone has fun and leaves happy."

At Noelle's frown, Colin reiterated. "It's a game, not a competition."

"If you say so. It would make more interesting footage if there was someone fighting for first place. Maybe a little rough and tumble over the trophy."

"Like the little brawl at the market?"

Noelle giggled. "We're still getting hits on that one."

"Yippee," he drawled.

But this time, instead of anger behind his words, Noelle could sense he was trying hard not to smile.

"You wouldn't want to go a few more rounds with the cousins, would you? Just for ratings?"

"Not a chance."

"Well, you can't blame a girl for trying."

Before she could convince Colin to tussle for ratings, their first putter showed up. Colin greeted the boy warmly. "Hey, Max." He turned to Noelle. "Max is the one who first told me about your show. He introduced me to your videos, and I have to admit, I wasn't thrilled to have you bring your particular *brand* to our small town.

Noelle winked at the boy. "Thanks, Max."

"I think you're great," he said. A blush rose to his cheeks. "I mean, I love your show."

"Well, that makes one of you," Noelle said, giving Colin a pointed look.

Max rushed to Colin's defense. "He said you were pretty!"

"Oh?" Noelle smiled at Colin. "Did you now?"

"No," he replied with a grin. "I said you were beautiful."

For once, Noelle was speechless. Luckily, Max chose that moment to call out, "Hey, I got a hole-in-one!"

Colin glanced at the boy. "You sure did. That gets you a coupon for a free slice of pizza from Taste of Italy."

"Woohoo!" Max made a victory gesture, then moved on to his next station.

The next few hours passed quickly with a steady stream of players. By the time they were done, the bag of coupons and candy was empty, and everyone left happy. Noelle and Colin worked together to dismantle the putt-putt and put away the balls and putters.

Noelle put her hands on her back and stretched, letting out a soft moan.

"Back hurting?" Colin asked.

"A bit achy. All this bending down to retrieve golf balls."

"I have an idea," Colin said. "You didn't happen to bring a bathing suit, did you?"

"To a winter carnival?"

"Right." He gave her an appraising look, measuring her from head to toe. "Angela leaves a bathing suit at my house that might fit you. Why don't you come over and use the hot tub? I promise it will relieve all your aches and pains."

Noelle started to object, then thought twice about it. Hot jets sounded delicious right about now. "Yes," she said. "I'd love that."

Colin's house was a short block away. Unlike the hunting cabin, however, it was decorated with a more modern flair, with dove gray walls, white furniture, and splashes of red accents. "Did you decorate this yourself?" she asked. It seemed to have a woman's touch, with potted plants, soft pillows, and framed artwork.

"Kelly, my assistant, was taking some design courses and asked if she could use my home as a model. To be honest, it was a blank slate. All I had in here was a television, kitchen table, and a recliner." He looked around. "I think she did a great job. Something I couldn't have accomplished in a million years."

"Yes." It seemed more personal somehow. She wondered if his assistant had ulterior motives for putting so much love and care into her boss's living quarters. She filed that information away in case it came in handy later.

Colin led her to a bedroom and gave her a two-piece bathing suit. "Do you think this will fit?"

"I think so."

Colin left her to change. The suit's bottom fit perfectly, with ties on each side so she could adjust it. The top was a little tight, showing a bit more cleavage than she was used to, but it would have to do. She covered up with the fluffy robe he'd left behind and put on a pair of slippers.

When she came out, Colin was in a matching robe. He'd set out a tray of cheese and crackers and two glasses of wine. She slipped off her robe and stepped into the hot tub. Sinking down into the bubby surface, she let out a soft moan. The jets hit her lower back in just the right places. "Are you coming in?" she asked.

He stared, then murmured, "You take my breath away."

Noelle's toes curled when she heard the longing in his voice. She had to turn away in case that same longing was reflected on her face.

Colin climbed into the hot tub and sat in the opposite corner. "How do those jets feel on your back?"

"Fabulous. Can I stay here?"

Colin chuckled. "As long as you'd like."

She almost made a comment about that being the suckiest proposal ever, but it hit too close to home. The truth was, she could actually see herself living here, making a home, and raising a family. She shook her head. It must be the wine.

Colin refilled both of their wine glasses as they watched the sunset. Steam rose from the water, making them feel alone in a hazy bubble. A light flurry drifted from the sky. She shifted, and her leg rubbed against his under the surface. It was a slow, sensual slide that Noelle felt straight to her core. It felt too good to pull away. Then his hand came to rest on her calf in a gentle caress. She bent her other knee and ran her toes along his inner thigh.

It felt wickedly erotic to be sitting calmly across from each other, drinking wine while their bodies slipped and slid skin-to-skin beneath the surface. She had to stop, or they'd end up in bed. But she didn't want to stop. She had to remind herself that she was here to do a job, not to seduce or be seduced.

She pulled her legs back to her corner, then put her empty glass on the side of the hot tub. "I really should be going," she said. "Gretchen and I still have work to do tonight."

"I understand." Colin stepped out of the hot tub first and grabbed her robe, allowing her to step into it.

She was both relieved and annoyed. He could have put up a bit of a fight. Just for appearances.

He wrapped the robe around her and held her close for a moment. She leaned back against his chest and let out a deep sigh. It would be so easy to turn around and kiss him, but she knew that one kiss wouldn't be enough. If she didn't leave now while she still had a modicum of reserve, they'd end up in bed and not surface until morning.

"Thank you," she said. "This was lovely."

"It's late," he said. "Why don't you let me walk you back to the lodge after you get changed?"

She didn't argue. Every stolen moment with him was one she would carry in her memory when she returned home.

## Chapter Eighteen

Colin stopped in the coffee shop the next morning and looked around, but there was no sign of Noelle. He went to the counter and asked Katie if Noelle had been in yet.

"Nope, haven't seen her."

Colin took his coffee and headed to his usual table in the back. Several people stopped by to talk about the festival. He was happy to hear that the cousins were working together to make their online shop a success. "We owe it all to Noelle," they told him.

Geoff stopped by the table. "I've decided what my sculpture will be," he said. "I think everyone will be surprised."

Colin had a bad feeling about that. He didn't like surprises, especially where the festival was concerned. But he was learning to let go and give up a little control wherever possible.

Max stopped by, and Colin grilled him about his grades. "How's that tutor doing?"

"She's okay. I might even pass algebra."

"You can do it." Colin raised his hand for a high five.

"So what's up?" He could see that Max had something else on his mind.

"I've been watching those videos. You know, Noelle's program?"

"Right."

"Yeah. She used to be kind of a..." Max's face flushed.

"Sarcastic?" Colin asked helpfully.

"Yeah. Sarcastic and kind of mean. But lately, she's just boring. I miss her old videos where she made fun of everything."

Colin found it amusing coming from the teenager. Of course, he'd find it boring when someone was acting like an adult.

After Max left, Colin finished his coffee and was about to leave when he saw Noelle and Gretchen come in. He waved them over. Gretchen gestured for Noelle to join Colin while she ordered their coffee.

Colin watched her saunter across the room. Every cell in his body rose to attention. He couldn't remember when a woman excited him as much, both physically and mentally. She had a hard shell exterior with a soft, sweet center. Unfortunately, not everyone got to see that sweetness inside.

She took a seat beside him and smiled. "What's on the agenda for today?"

"More of the usual," he said. "Plus, the ice sculptures will be revealed today."

Noelle lifted an eyebrow. "Will there be time to go snowmobiling?"

The way she said it sent his mind reeling in erotic directions. "Perhaps we can squeeze some snowmobiling time in."

Gretchen came to the table carrying coffee, putting an

end to what may or may not have been a subtle flirtation. Or maybe that was only in his mind.

Unfortunately, he didn't have time for a one-on-one conversation with Noelle because she and Gretchen put their heads together and started talking business. Trying to gain Noelle's attention, he brought up his conversation with Max. "He said he likes the old Noelle better than the new, kinder version."

"That seems to be the consensus these days," Gretchen muttered.

Noelle pursed her lips. "Ouch."

"Come on," Colin said. "You're not worried about what a teenager thinks, are you? They like dark and irreverent. That's what being a teenager is all about."

Noelle gave him a thoughtful look, but he could tell she was worried. He wanted to reassure her, but this was well out of his field of expertise. It was obvious she and Gretchen had work to do, and he was just in the way.

In a final attempt to get her attention, he gestured to her cup. "How's that coffee?"

Her lips turned up in a slow, sexy smile. "I've had better."

"There's more where that came from."

"I'll take you up on that." She paused, then added, "After we get some work done."

He could take a hint. "I guess I'll be getting along," he said, hoping Noelle would stop him, but she smiled and waved.

"See you later," she said, then bent over the papers Gretchen spread on the table.

He nodded, then turned to leave, feeling a bit disappointed. At least he'd see her later today. And it was just as well. He had work to do.

Back at the office, he caught his assistant watching

videos of Noelle. She looked up and frowned. "I'm not so sure I like her," Kelly said.

Colin nodded. "She can be hard to take."

"I can't tell if she's really mean or just putting on an act."

"I think it's more than an act, Kelly. I think it's a persona she uses to protect herself."

Kelly raised an eyebrow at him.

"Look," he continued, "I do know her videos are bringing in more people. And more people means more donations. With her help, we should make our fundraising goal and then some."

"And then she goes home, right?"

Colin nodded. Kelly was right. Once the festival ended, Noelle would be leaving, but he didn't want to think about that. He wanted to enjoy every minute of the next few days while she was still here.

On impulse, he texted Noelle and asked if she wanted to join him for lunch. She replied with a thumbs-up emoji, and he texted that he'd pick her up at the lodge at twelve. In a better mood, he was able to concentrate on his work.

Until he heard a groan from outside his office. He rushed out to the hallway and found Kelly bent over with her arms around her stomach. "I think it's time," she said. She moaned as another pain shot through her. She gave Colin a beseeching look. "It's too early. The baby's not due for another month."

Colin draped an arm around her waist and helped her to his car. Once she was safely inside, he told her to text her husband and have him meet them at the hospital, and then Colin drove as fast as the speed limit would allow.

The hospital was only ten minutes away, but it was the longest ten minutes of his life. "Almost there," he said, trying to comfort her as her moans grew louder and longer.

## Chapter Nineteen

Noelle and Gretchen were just finishing up at the coffee shop when Stuart texted, requesting another video meeting. Noelle rubbed her eyes and let out a sigh. "I don't have time for this."

"Maybe we can get it over with quickly."

They picked up their things and headed back to the lodge. They'd been in town less than a week, but it already felt like home … or the home she'd always wished she'd had growing up. The streetlights were decorated with snowflakes, candles, and wreaths that glowed brightly at night. Storefronts were draped in balsam and ribbons, with movable Christmas scenes to delight children and adults alike. Noelle felt as if she'd landed smack in the middle of a Christmas movie.

Looking around, Gretchen asked, "What do you think they do when Christmas is over?"

"Maybe they celebrate Christmas all year long?"

"That wouldn't surprise me."

Noelle looked around at the happy little houses with their colored lights. "Could you imagine living here?"

"You know," Gretchen said. "I think I could. Weird, huh?"

"Yeah. Weird." And yet, the little town was growing on her. So was its mayor.

Not as pleasant was their video call with Stuart. He pulled no punches. "If you don't get your engagement numbers back up, Noelle, your job is decidedly in jeopardy."

God, he was like a broken record. Noelle wasn't sure whether he was really concerned about their subscribers or if he just enjoyed threatening her job. The call ended on a disheartening note.

Noelle sat back, stretching the kinks out of her back. "So where do we go from here?"

"I think we need to finish with a bang."

"Go big or go home, right?"

"Right."

They threw out ideas, but nothing seemed like the solution they were looking for.

Noelle bit her bottom lip. "What do you think about what Colin said this morning?"

"About that teenager's opinion?"

"Yeah."

Gretchen took her time answering. "I think he has a point. You've built a reputation on a certain irreverent attitude laced with a healthy dose of sarcasm. You can't just change that overnight without disappointing a few people."

"According to Stuart, it's more than just a few people."

Gretchen looked thoughtful. "You know, I think Colin is a good influence, but we have to find a way to cater to the new subscribers while getting some of your zing back to please the regulars."

Noelle nodded.

"Leave it to me," Gretchen said. "I may have a few ideas."

After Gretchen left, Noelle pulled up some of the footage from the day before. Seeing Colin brought a smile to her face. He handled the activities like a maestro. Everywhere he went, he was treated with good humor and respect. What caught her attention was the way his gaze followed her when she wasn't looking. Every woman dreamed of being looked at that way, with an equal measure of attraction and desire. Was it any wonder she was too distracted to come up with snarky comments?

Did she care? Not as much as she would have a week ago. Right now, the only thing she cared about was spending more time with Colin. She shut down her computer and checked her watch. It was almost noon, and knowing Colin would be here to pick her up soon brought a smile to her face.

She still had a few hours to catch up on email and knock a few things off her to-do list. When the time drew closer, she put her hair up, added a touch of make-up, and went down to the lobby to wait for Colin. She pulled one of the books she'd purchased at the bookstore out of her tote bag and sat in front of the fire to read while she waited. It was nice to be able to sit down and read a book for pleasure.

She'd read several chapters before she looked at the clock and realized Colin was half an hour late. Maybe she'd misunderstood and was supposed to meet him in town? She checked her phone, but there was no text from him.

It wasn't the first time she'd been stood up. There was a time back in high school when she thought the boy she had a crush on had said he'd pick her up to go roller skating, but he'd never showed. She went to the roller rink and found him skating with another girl. She'd cried for a week.

She wasn't that young girl anymore. She'd grown up — and grown stronger. No man was worth her tears. Not even a hot mayor.

~

COLIN AND KELLY'S HUSBAND, Arthur, stood when the doctor came into the waiting room. "She's going to be fine," the doctor said. "It was just Braxton Hicks contractions."

"Is that serious?" Arthur asked.

"It's actually quite common. You've probably heard it called false labor. Feels like the real thing, but it's not."

"But the baby's okay?"

"Absolutely fine. So is Mom, and she can return to her normal routine."

Colin spoke up. "I think she should rest at home. We can get by without her."

Just then, Kelly was wheeled out of the examination room. "I heard that," she said. "You're not getting rid of me that easily."

"But…"

"The doctor said I can get back to my normal routine, and my normal routine is in the office. At least until the festival is over."

Colin started to argue, but Kelly stood firm. "I'm at the office until the festival is *over*. Then I'll take a Christmas break. We'll discuss my work schedule after the new year."

Arthur glanced at Colin. "Never argue with a pregnant woman." He stopped, then added, "Or any woman, for that matter."

Colin started to laugh, then remembered his date with Noelle. He glanced at his watch. "Uh oh. I'm late."

He leaned down and gave Kelly a hug, then shook Arthur's hand. "You got this?"

"I do. And thanks again."

Colin left the hospital and rushed to the lodge. There was no sign of Noelle in the lobby. He ran to her room and knocked on the door, but she didn't answer. He texted her, but there was no reply. His shoulders slumped.

He'd messed up.

# Chapter Twenty

Noelle walked around the marketplace, making small talk with the vendors while keeping an eye out for Colin. She walked by the community room, but no sign of him. She tried to tell herself she wasn't really looking for him, just wanted to make plans for the rest of the filming. She had a schedule to keep.

Plus, she was getting worried. It wasn't like him to miss an appointment. She didn't really want to call it a date. Something important must have come up. Maybe a gingerbread house had collapsed, or one of the carolers had laryngitis.

Her last stop was the skating rink. She sat on a bench and watched the skaters, smiling to herself. The scene looked so much like the snow globe she treasured from her grandfather and brought back sweet memories. She'd spent so long focusing on the bad memories that she'd almost forgotten the good ones. Mornings when her grandfather made her special pancakes with smiley faces. The old tire swing he'd hung from a hundred-year-old oak tree in his backyard. And the hugs. He was the best hugger.

The truth was, after her mother left, her grandfather tried to make Christmas special, but she was so miserable and angry that nothing would have made her happy. She wished she'd appreciated his efforts. She wished she'd been more grateful that he'd stepped up to be the parent her own parents couldn't be.

Suddenly, Angela was beside her, a comforting arm around her shoulder. "Are you okay, honey?"

Noelle nodded and wiped a tear from her cheek. "Just missing my grandfather."

Angela pulled her close. It felt like her grandfather was sending her a hug from heaven. She rested her head on the woman's shoulder momentarily, basking in the warmth. Then she took a deep breath and sat up straight. That was enough wallowing in self-pity. She had a job to do. "Have you seen Colin?" she asked.

Angela nodded. "Oh, he rushed Kelly to the hospital. They thought she was in labor, but it turned out to be a false alarm. You might try his office, but I don't think he's back yet." She gestured with a turn of her head. "Why don't you head over that way?"

Noelle stood, but before leaving, she reached out and squeezed Angela's hand. "Thank you."

She strolled casually toward the mayor's office. She'd been running on a hamster wheel for so long that she didn't know what it was like to take her time and enjoy everything — the crisp air, the sound of laughter on the wind, and the anticipation of meeting a man who just might change her life for the better.

And knowing she hadn't been stood up added to her sense of well-being. She'd been upset about what may have kept him from their appointment, but rushing his assistant to the hospital was a good reason to forget he was supposed to pick her up for lunch.

She saw him coming out of the building before he noticed she was there. She admired the way his jeans fit, not too tight but snug in the right places, enough to make her mind wander in all sorts of directions. When he spotted her, a smile of delight lit up his face and made her tingle all over.

He started apologizing before he even reached her. "I'm sorry I missed our luncheon date, but Kelly—"

Noelle stopped him. "Angela told me. I understand completely."

He let out a sigh of relief. "When I couldn't find you at the lodge, I was afraid you'd be angry. I tried to text."

Noelle laughed. "I turned my phone off. Stuart was being annoying, and I wanted to enjoy the day without feeling guilty about work."

He took her hand. "I approve. No work talk for either one of us."

"Really?"

He took his phone out of his pocket and turned it off. "There. Now we have a few hours to ourselves, and no one can interrupt."

Their gazes spoke volumes for them. Then, they both spoke at once. Colin laughed. "You first."

"I was wondering if we could go snowmobiling or something."

He lifted an eyebrow. "Or something?"

"Actually, I was hoping we could go to your cabin. I could use a good cup of espresso."

"Is that all I am to you? A barista? Do you only want me for my espresso?"

"That and the hot tub."

He laughed again. "I feel so used." His eyes flashed an invitation. "Let's go. It might be quicker by car. I had the driveway plowed."

He didn't have to ask twice. They walked to his car and were at the cabin in less than ten minutes. He opened the door and turned on the Christmas tree lights. The sight of the place made Noelle feel warm inside. Christmas was growing on her. She looked at each ornament, remembering what each represented in Colin's life. She focused on the ice-skating ornament. It meant she was important in his life, too.

"I'll get the coffee started," he said. "Did you end up having lunch?"

"No, I was saving myself for you."

His eyes widened.

"I mean…" She felt color rush to her cheeks. "I meant for my appetite. For lunch." She couldn't seem to put a whole sentence together.

"Lunch," he said. "Let me see what I can whip up."

He went into the kitchen, and Noelle wiped her forehead. For someone who was normally so in control, she sure couldn't seem to put two sentences together when Colin was around lately. She walked around the room, touching books on the shelf and games gathered on the card table. She tried to imagine what family days were like when Colin was growing up. She wondered if they actually did any hunting at the cabin.

When Colin came back with two cups of espresso, that was the first thing she asked him. "Do you actually hunt here? I don't see any guns or anything."

Colin handed her one of the coffee cups. "Not in years. My grandfather used to hunt. I remember eating venison at his house until I found out he'd killed Bambi for our dinner. I cried for a week." He laughed. "I don't think my grandfather did any hunting after that. And I haven't eaten venison since."

"Well, that explains it," she said, pointing to the Bambi ornament.

Colin wrapped an arm around her shoulder. "Can't put one past you, can I?"

"Well, there is one I've been wondering about." Was she being too forward to ask? "This one." She pointed to an ornament she didn't remember going on the tree. Inside a heart-shaped frame was a picture of a woman with a kind face and a wide, welcoming smile.

"My mother," Colin said, his voice tender. "Before she got sick."

She took the ornament off the tree and studied it. "She's beautiful."

"Inside and out."

She handed the ornament to Colin. "Tell me about her."

He blinked and cradled it in his palm. "Wow, where to start? She was fun-loving and enjoyed playing games and sports. She gave her all to the job without taking anything away from our family." He gave a wry grin. "Something Angela keeps telling me I need to learn."

"She says you work too hard. But..." She gave him a knowing look. "I think that would change if you had a family to come home to. Like your mother did. Maybe you wouldn't pour everything you had into your work."

"She did it all, though. She was a great mother and a great mayor. I have big shoes to fill."

Noelle took a sip of her coffee, trying to find the words that would get through to him without sounding insincere. "I think you're the only one who feels that pressure. Everyone loves you, and everyone I speak to praises your work. No one compares you to your mother. Or anyone else, for that matter."

Colin took a deep breath, then released it slowly as if

dropping a heavy weight from his shoulders. He brushed his fingers over his mother's picture, then placed it back on the tree. "I hope you're right."

They stood there for a moment, both staring at the tree. "Best tree ever," Colin said.

"Is it?"

He laughed. "We say that every year."

"You and your traditions."

"Stick with me, babe. We can make some traditions of our own."

"Hmmm." She gave a low hum, which could have been interpreted either way. Then, she lifted her face and sniffed the air. "What's that smell?"

"Oh!" Colin rushed into the kitchen. "I put a frozen lasagna in the oven."

Noelle followed him in. He opened the oven and waved away a fog of steam. She grabbed a set of potholders off the counter and handed them to Colin before he could reach in and burn his hands.

He lifted the lasagna out of the oven. Other than a few dark edges, it looked delicious, and the aroma made her taste buds sing. "I hope you like lasagna," he said.

"It's one of my favorites." That was true. Who didn't love a combination of carbs and cheese?

"Great." He cut two squares of hot, gooey lasagna and placed them on plates.

Noelle carried the dishes to the table while Colin opened a bottle of red. He poured them each a glass, then raised his for a toast. "To Christmas," he said.

"To Christmas." And Noelle found, to her surprise, that she meant it.

They ate in companionable silence. When they were finished, they stood at the sink washing their dishes, silverware, and wine glasses. It all felt very … domestic. She felt like she'd been lifted out of her real world and plunked down in the center of some 50s sitcom.

When the kitchen was cleaned, Colin checked his watch and grimaced. "Guess our phone-free time is up."

Noelle shrugged, half-jokingly saying, "Maybe we should leave our phones off all night and stay here in our little bubble."

"I would love that, but…"

Her heart fell. "But?"

"But I talked with that travel website, TripTips, earlier this morning. Your videos caught their attention. They have a photographer and journalist on the way this after-noon and want to interview me about the festival."

Noelle was happy she had a part in bringing more attention to the town's festival but was also a little annoyed. This was *her* project. She didn't want to share, but more publicity would be good for the town and help them reach their fundraising goal.

"That's wonderful," she said, hoping it sounded sincere.

"Yeah, but honestly, it makes me a little nervous. I almost wish I hadn't agreed to an interview."

Noelle heard the nervousness in his voice and tried to reassure him. "I was just going over the videos from yester-day. You look great on camera, and you speak with author-ity. You're a natural."

"You think?"

"Believe me. I've interviewed my share of people who stuttered and stammered and laced their sentences with 'ums' and 'likes.' You're a dream to work with."

He raised an eyebrow. "A dream, huh?"

"More like a nightmare," she quipped with a grin.

He burst out laughing. "Who says you've lost your edge?"

They drove to the festival grounds and parked near the community hall. When Colin reached out for her hand, she didn't pull away. "So when are these travel people supposed to arrive?"

He glanced at his watch. "In an hour or so. They want to be here for the ice carving contest."

"That sounds like a good place to start. For the record, we'll be covering the ice carving contest as well."

"Of course."

"Too bad we won't have time to go snowmobiling." She wasn't sure when "snowmobiling" became a code word for potentially making out.

Colin emitted a low, throaty growl that went directly to her center. "We'll make time later."

It sounded like a challenge. And she was always up for a challenge.

~

NOELLE ARRIVED early to begin filming for the ice carving contest. Gretchen was already there, but she was focused on Geoff and offering him encouragement. It seemed he was suffering from a case of nerves. He stood next to his draped sculpture and kept glancing between his sculpture and Colin.

The men from the travel site had arrived, and Noelle watched as they interviewed Colin.

"This town and the people we serve are special to me," he said. "The money we bring in from the festival will go toward a new roof for the school and repairing water damage from a burst pipe at the library."

The interviewer from the travel site leaned in. "How close are you to meeting your goal?"

Colin gestured to the giant candy cane fundraising

board. The red and white stripes were only three-quarters of the way to the top. "We're a little short," he said. "But we still have a few days left in the festival."

Noelle stood on the sidelines as he talked about the town he loved and how much good would come from the money raised at the festival. He glanced over at Noelle, who gave him the thumbs-up sign.

She found herself following Colin's interview word for word. She felt just as invested in the festival's success as the rest of the town. It wasn't just a job anymore. It felt personal.

She glanced at the candy cane fundraising board. What if they didn't make their goal? Not only that but even if they raised enough money for the school roof and library basement, what then? Would they even have enough money in their budget for the rest of the year? How do you even begin to run a town without money coming in?

She had no doubt Colin would continue on as mayor without receiving a paycheck. He was that dedicated. But what about the rest of the people on staff? And what happens when there's another emergency?

She had an idea, but it would take a little research. She'd have to cancel her snowmobiling plans and get to work on it as soon as possible. But right now, there was the ice carving contest. Colin was explaining to the travel people how it would work. "First prize is a gift certificate for six months of pottery studio use, including clay and use of the kiln, donated by Beverly Flynn at the Pottery Club."

Beverly stood to a round of applause.

"The runner-up gift certificate has been donated by Katie Flynn, Beverly's daughter, who you know as our own coffee barista at the Coffee Cafe. And that's good for six months of coffee on the house."

Another round of applause as Katie stood up and took a bow. Noelle leaned over and whispered to Gretchen, "If I'd known that was the prize, I'd have sculpted something myself."

"Oh? Like what?"

"I don't know. An ice cube shaped to look like an ice cube?"

"Yep, that would be a winner for sure."

They went live when the judging started. Noelle handled the microphone while Gretchen filmed. She ran commentary and let the TripTips people step up and interview the sculptors.

The first entry was unveiled to reveal an ice snowman. "As you can see," Noelle spoke to the camera, "here we have your typical Frosty the Snowman carving, complete with a corncob pipe and a button nose."

Colin studied the carving, walking around the back and looking at it from every angle. "What was your inspiration for this ice carving?" he asked the artist.

"Well, when I was a kid, the best part of winter was building snowmen in our backyard."

Noelle rolled her eyes at the camera as they moved on to the next sculpture, which was unveiled to reveal an intricate ice snowflake lit from below with LED lights that made it sparkle from within.

"That's very pretty," Noelle said to the camera. "I'm not sure how long the ice will last with those lights on it, but whatever."

The next carving to be unveiled was a life-sized nutcracker. It looked a bit like SpongeBob SquarePants, but Noelle didn't mention that. The sculptor *was a young woman who said her mother collected nutcrackers, and they watched the movie The Nutcracker every Christmas Eve.*

Noelle turned to the camera and shrugged.

The last entry was Geoff's. After talking to him, Noelle was curious to see what he came up with besides the traditional Christmas fare. When the carving was unveiled, there was dead silence.

"What is this?" Colin asked.

"Well, this is a reindeer." He gestured to the sculpture of a woman lying on the ground with hoof marks on her back. "And that's grandma. She got run over…"

"I know the song," Colin said, his voice tight.

"Yeah, we sang it at karaoke. That's what gave me the idea." His voice quivered. "See, it's a metaphor about family unity, for appreciating our loved ones, especially over the holidays."

Colin quickly moved on. Noelle thought it was funny, but it was obvious by the clench of Colin's jaw and the tightness of his lips that he was angry. Geoff noticed as well because he hung his head and tried to appear invisible. Noelle gestured to Gretchen to stop filming. As much as she wanted to keep it real, she didn't want to embarrass either of them.

The rest of the contest was uneventful. Noelle kept glancing at Colin, but he avoided her gaze. In the end, it was the illuminated snowflake that won first place. Geoff came in last. They finished filming, and Gretchen went off to comfort him while Noelle stayed behind.

She hung back until the TripTips people left, then joined Colin. He took a deep breath, then spoke in a low voice. "Did you encourage him to do this?"

"What? He wanted to do something non-traditional. I thought it was funny."

"He made me a laughingstock in front of the TripTips people."

Noelle could see he was upset, but it seemed like such a small thing. Maybe it was the stress he was under, but he seemed to be taking it personally. "His heart was in the right place," she said, defending Geoff's artistic choice.

"So you knew about this?"

"Well, I didn't know exactly what he'd planned, just that he wanted to do something less traditional. I think 'outside the box' were his exact words." She could see Colin wasn't buying it. "Look," she said. "There's such a thing as artistic license. You can't control everyone and everything."

"I did a fine job until you got here."

"Well, lucky for you, I'll be leaving soon." With that, she turned on her heel and followed Gretchen.

When she reached Geoff's carving, she admired the detail, right down to the grandma's knitting needles. "That's amazing," she told Geoff.

He shrugged. "I came in last."

"Well, you know Colin has a more traditional idea of what an ice sculpture should look like. That doesn't mean there's anything wrong with yours."

"Yeah," Gretchen added. "Beauty is in the eyes of the beholder."

Geoff gave her a grateful smile. "Thanks."

It wasn't long before Colin joined them. "I'm sorry," he said. "I was so worried about making a good impression on those TripTips people that it clouded my judgment." He glanced at the sculpture. "It caught me by surprise."

Geoff lifted one shoulder and gave a half-hearted smile. "Yeah, I guess it was a little unpredictable. But that's what I was going for."

"Would have been nice if you'd given me a heads-up," Colin said, putting an arm around Geoff's shoulder.

"Next time."

Colin turned to Noelle. "I have a few things to take

care of at the office, but if you're free, would you join me for dinner?"

Noelle tipped her head thoughtfully. "I think I can fit you in."

"How do you feel about tacos?"

"I can taco 'em or leave 'em."

Colin groaned and shook his head. "That was terrible."

Noelle giggled. "You're right, but it was short notice, and I didn't have time to edit."

"Is that what you do with your videos? Edit until you get them, right?"

Noelle gave him a long look, not sure if he was serious or not. "That's my job," she said.

He nodded, then dropped the subject. "It's Taco Tuesday at Blitzen's. How does six o'clock sound?"

Sounded unappetizing. She wasn't a fan of tacos. But she was a fan of Colin. "I'll meet you there."

# Chapter Twenty-One

Colin spent the next few hours reviewing paperwork in the office, but thoughts of Noelle kept interrupting his flow. She wasn't like anyone he'd known before. She kept him off balance, sweet one minute and spicy the next. He gave up trying to concentrate and decided to go to Blitzen's early and wait for Noelle.

On his way out the door, he ran into Max. "Hey," Max said. "Thanks for talking to Noelle."

"Hmmm. Why's that?"

"She's back to her old self again." Max pushed some buttons on his phone, then held it up for Colin to see.

He was surprised to see a video of them at the ice skating rink. Hadn't she said she wouldn't film that day? And then he heard her voiceover. Yeah, the old, snarky Noelle was back with a vengeance. Not only was she blasting away at all things Christmas, but she was even reusing some of her old jokes. At least be original!

The more he watched, the angrier he got. She knew how much this festival meant, not only to him but to the entire town. Her comments were mean-spirited and down-right disrespectful.

Colin's stomach dropped as he listened to her make fun of him during a moment that had felt really heartfelt and sincere. When he leaned in and gave her a hug, her voice-over stated, "People kiss, then break up, then make up, then kiss some more. And just when you think it's going to be some great romance, someone dies."

What? Was she talking about his mother? Was she really using their personal and private conversation to entertain her viewers? She wasn't the person he thought she was.

"You know," she continued as she and Colin leaned closer on the screen, "there are people who say *Romeo and Juliet* is a romance. It's not. It's a tragedy, and so is this."

Colin struck his fist on the desk. Why would she have acted like she wasn't filming if this had been her plan all along? He was justifiably angry, but more than anything, he felt hurt. That night had been special for him. He thought it was special for her as well. Not just an opportunity to make fun of things that were important to him.

She was a fraud.

He went to Blitzen's, his mood darkening with each step. When he walked through the door, he spotted Noelle sitting at the bar, one leg draped over the other. He tried not to let the sight of her dampen his anger.

He stepped up close, letting her feel the heat of his anger. "I saw the video."

She blinked, but he wasn't about to let her innocent act fool him again. "What video?" she asked.

"The one at the ice rink. You said you weren't going to film that night. But it was just another opportunity for you to mock me and everything I believe in."

"I don't—"

"And you lied to me," he said, not letting her get a word in to defend herself. "You lied to me, then used what I thought was a meaningful conversation against me. You used me to get ratings."

"I would never—"

But he wasn't listening. "I wish you'd never come to Evergreen Creek," he said.

Noelle stood and faced him eye to eye. "I have no idea what you're talking about."

"Yeah, right." He turned on his heel and walked out before he could say something he'd regret.

Noelle watched him go, more confused than ever. She took out her phone and pulled up the channel, surprised to see a new video posted. She watched in horror as their most tender moments were turned into something shallow and paltry. It was her voice, but she didn't record this voiceover. Most of it was cut and pasted from her rant about that stupid movie, *Over the Rainbow Bridge*.

This wasn't her doing. She recognized comments she'd made in other podcasts that were obviously cut and pasted into this video as well. The only one with the capacity to do that was Gretchen. But why?

She grabbed her purse, wiping tears from her eyes, then walked out the door. At least she didn't have to pretend to like tacos.

Despite the mess this had become, she still wanted to put her plan into motion. She hadn't decided what she'd do after that. She set up a FundEvergreenCreek page and posted a text message to her subscribers.

. . .

*I ᴋɴᴏᴡ you're all invested in the Evergreen Creek Christmas Festival. While our videos have brought in many visitors to the festival, they still haven't reached their goal to build a new roof on the school and repair water damage to the library, not to mention keeping the town afloat for the upcoming year.*

*Here's where you come in. I know not all of you can make the trip to Evergreen Creek, but you can show your support from the comfort of your own home. If each of my subscribers makes just a one-dollar donation to the FundEvergreenCreek page, not only will they reach their goals this year, but they'll have enough reserves in their budget to keep the town solvent for the next several years. Think of it. Just one dollar can save an entire town.*

*Are you with me?*

Wɪᴛʜ ᴏᴠᴇʀ ᴀ ᴍɪʟʟɪᴏɴ sᴜʙsᴄʀɪʙᴇʀs, Noelle knew that if only half of them donated a single dollar, she'd raise enough for Evergreen Creek to rebuild the town and bring businesses back to the area.

# Chapter Twenty-Two

NOELLE LEFT messages on Colin's voicemail, but there was no response. She tried calling his office, but Kelly informed her that Colin wasn't taking calls. Noelle suspected that Kelly was screening his calls to protect him. Surely, everyone had seen her video by now, and the ranks were closing around Colin, protecting their mayor.

She sent him a text explaining that she wasn't responsible for that video, but if he saw it, he didn't reply. She went to his office, but Angela headed her off, saying Colin was in a meeting.

Noelle sighed. "Tell him it wasn't me."

Angela nodded, but Noelle wasn't sure she'd say anything. Obviously, she was protective of Colin, and Noelle was an outsider who'd turned their beloved town into a laughingstock.

Walking back to the lodge, every place she passed held memories of times with Colin. It seemed unfair that he wouldn't give her the chance to explain. Had she meant so little to him that he could just write her off so quickly without an explanation?

Back at the lodge, she confronted Gretchen. "I hate that Colin thinks I was behind that video."

Gretchen had the decency to look ashamed. "I simply did what you weren't willing to do. And it worked. Our ratings went through the roof. I tried to call you, but—"

"My phone was turned off." Noelle let out a deep sigh. She never should have turned her phone off when they were working. It was as much her own fault as Gretchen's. "Colin thinks I betrayed him. He won't even give me a chance to explain."

"I'm sorry."

Noelle couldn't stay angry at Gretchen. She'd done what she thought the company needed. A few weeks ago, Noelle would have done the same thing. She'd learned to separate personal desires from business decisions. That strategy had been thrown out the window when Colin entered the picture. She'd grown soft.

"I can't stay here," she said. "Everything reminds me of Colin. Everywhere I go, everyone I see. I'm the villain here, and Colin is the small-town hero. There's no place for me in Evergreen Creek."

Gretchen remained silent. Whether she agreed or not, Noelle knew it was her decision to make. She tried to focus on the job at hand, but her heart wasn't in it. She just wanted to run far away. It hurt too much to stay.

When Gretchen left, she called Stuart. He answered her call with a brusque hello.

"I can't finish the assignment," she said without preamble. "I need some time off."

"We've committed to four more episodes."

"I know," Noelle said. "And Gretchen is willing to finish up here. She's already taken the lead in filming and editing. She doesn't need me here to wrap things up."

"Okay," Stuart said. "Take some time off and get your

head together. We'll figure something out while you're gone." His voice softened. "Get some rest and take care of yourself, Noelle."

Noelle noticed he didn't say her job would be there when she returned. That was something to think about another day.

She spent the next few hours packing all her clothes and equipment. She'd run out of space in her suitcase after buying so many trinkets at the marketplace. Each one made her smile and remember the person who sold it to her. How easy it would be to live here permanently and be embraced as a friend by these people.

No, she couldn't think like that. She had an apartment to get back to, a cat to spoil, and hopefully, there'd be a job waiting for her when she returned. This was just a small interlude in her life, one she'd look back on with fond memories.

Once she'd packed everything and double-checked the room, she called for a driver to take her to the airport. She'd already said her goodbyes to Gretchen. There was no one else she needed to see other than Colin, and he was avoiding her like the Christmas plague.

It was a short flight to New York City. She called for a taxi and watched the streets as they passed. For all the festive decorations, she couldn't find the spirit of Christmas she'd felt in Evergreen Creek. Once she was home, she unlocked the door to her apartment. It felt bare, without a single touch of Christmas. It hadn't bothered her until now. She thought about the houses back in Evergreen Creek, lit up and decorated to the nines. Her apartment was a pale comparison as if Christmas had never existed.

Colin was right. She *was* a Grinch.

She dropped her bags, took off her jacket, and tried to get comfortable. She felt a sudden urge for hot chocolate and gingerbread. Silly. As hard as she tried, it didn't feel like coming home. Her apartment was cold, quiet, and lonely. She picked up her grandfather's snow globe and shook it, remembering her time at the skating rink with Colin. An ache of yearning filled her heart. If only she could go back in time and explain everything to him. Not only her lifelong fear of abandonment but how he'd helped her face it and begin to feel joy again. He'd made her believe in love, family, and the spirit of Christmas. Maybe if she had, he would have believed her when she said there was no way she'd say the things he'd heard on the altered video.

She wandered around her apartment. Maybe she'd go out and buy a few decorations tomorrow. Perhaps even a small tree. She thought about Colin's massive tree and the ice-skating ornament hanging on it. Her vision blurred as hot tears filled her eyes. Everything he'd said about the meaning of Christmas and family and long-held traditions rushed through her memories. Family. He said that was the true meaning of Christmas.

Noelle picked up her phone and dialed her mother's number. At the sound of her mother's voice, she felt weepy. "Hey," she said. "Remember what I said about making new memories?"

"Yes." The word was drawn out like a question.

"Can we start now?" Noelle asked.

"Whatever you want," her mother replied. "Just say the word."

Noelle was forming a plan. If it worked, it just might fix everything.

## Chapter Twenty-Three

COLIN FOCUSED hard on his work. The harder he focused, the harder it was not to let thoughts of Noelle spoil his mood. Anger and betrayal formed a hard pit in his stomach every time he thought of the video she'd posted. He'd fallen so hard that he couldn't see that she'd been using him the whole time just to boost her ratings. He was an idiot.

As hard as he tried not to think about her, everywhere he went carried memories of Noelle. Even the coffee shop no longer held appeal. The coffee tasted bitter without her by his side. And he was pretty sure he wouldn't be able to set foot in the cabin again.

She hadn't shown up for the tree-lighting ceremony the night before, and as mad as he was, he couldn't help being disappointed. He'd searched for her in a sea of faces, but she was nowhere to be found.

He picked up a packet of pamphlets to drop off at the lodge, but in his heart, he knew it was just an excuse. He hoped to run into Noelle. Maybe there was a way they could patch things up. Maybe he'd been too quick to jump to conclusions.

Opening the lodge door, he was surprised to see Gretchen waiting in the lobby with her suitcases.

"Are you leaving?" he asked.

She nodded. "We have everything we need to finish up."

"But Santa arrives tonight with Christmas gifts for the children. That would be the perfect ending for your videos."

Gretchen shrugged.

Colin looked around. "Is Noelle coming down too?"

Gretchen shook her head. "She left already. Yesterday."

He felt a stab of pain in his heart. She couldn't even see the project through? Had she left without saying good-bye? "I guess once the project was over, she didn't need to be here anymore."

"No," Gretchen said. "She left because you wouldn't answer her calls or respond to her texts. She left because you believed the worst of her and didn't give her a chance to explain."

Colin was at a loss for words. What did Gretchen mean he didn't answer her calls? She'd left one voicemail saying it wasn't her fault, that she hadn't uploaded that video. He hadn't responded because he'd hoped they could talk face-to-face.

"And for the record," Gretchen said, stepping into the waiting taxi. "I was the one who cut and pasted her comments into that last video and uploaded it. She knew nothing about it."

Colin's stomach dropped. Noelle had been telling the truth. He felt like a cad for not believing her. As Gretchen's taxi pulled away, Colin beat himself up for how he behaved. He went to the only place he could think of for advice and comfort.

Angela opened the door, took one look at his face, and gestured him inside. "Coffee?"

"You wouldn't have anything stiffer, would you?"

"I can put a shot of Irish cream in it."

"Sounds good. Hold the coffee," he said with a grin.

"That bad, huh?"

He followed Angela into the kitchen and took a seat. She poured them each a cup of coffee and brought out the bottle of Irish cream.

Colin poured a shot of courage into his coffee, then unloaded to Angela. "Noelle left."

Angela nodded. "I saw her get into a cab yesterday."

"You didn't say anything."

"I wasn't sure if you wanted to know. You seemed pretty upset with her."

"Yeah, after I saw that video, I was furious. I couldn't believe she'd made a laughingstock of me and the entire town. She said she knew nothing about it, but I didn't believe her."

"And now you do?"

"Gretchen admitted she did the whole thing to raise the ratings."

Angela added a shot of Irish cream to her own coffee. "Well, it didn't hurt us. We ended up making our fundraising goals and a whole lot more for a cushion."

"Seriously? Since yesterday?"

Angela shrugged her shoulders. "There was a huge jump in donations yesterday. Not sure where they came from, but it put us over the top. As a matter of fact, it almost doubled our goals."

Colin shook his head. There was something off about

that, and he had a feeling Noelle had something to do with the sudden surge of donations.

"So," Angela said. "No harm done."

"Except for my ego."

"Egos heal. You can still make things right if you want to."

"I do."

"If this thing with Noelle is good, you should fight for it. Don't let your pride get in the way." She punched his shoulder. "And stop being a horse's ass."

Colin grinned. "I'll try to do better."

Still curious about the sudden uptick in donations, Colin decided to ask the expert on all things Noelle-related. He dialed Max's number. "Hey, Max. We seem to have a lot of donations coming in. Do you know anything about that?"

"Sure do," Max said. "You've gotta see it to believe it. Meet me at the coffee shop, and I'll show you."

Ten minutes later, Colin was looking over Max's shoulder at what seemed to be a donation site. The page was headlined *FundEvergreenCreek*, and it looked as if donations were pouring in by the minute.

"What is this?"

Max smiled. "Noelle set this up to raise donations from her subscribers. She said if everyone donated a dollar, there'd be enough to meet our goals and then some." He pointed to the screen. "Look at that!

The figures were higher than Colin could have imagined.

"Hey," Max said. "With all these donations, maybe we could build a skatepark."

"We have more important things to worry about than skateboarding," Colin said with a smile. "But if these figures are right, I'll put it on the agenda." He watched more donations pour in. "You said she asked everyone to donate a dollar?"

"Yep."

"And how many subscribers would you say she has?"

Max lifted one shoulder. "I don't know. A million?"

Colin shook his head in amazement. If even a portion of those subscribers donated a dollar, they wouldn't have to worry about the treasury for years to come.

# Chapter Twenty-Four

GRETCHEN GOT BACK in town just in time for another general meeting at Your Social Media Source. Noelle watched as Gretchen revealed the latest video with comedic outtakes of Christmas Town USA. The background music played "Mr. Grinch" over a montage of Noelle rolling her eyes or mugging for the camera.

"I love it," Stuart said.

Noelle couldn't join in the laughter. Yes, it was fun, at her expense, and harkened back to that snarky, sometimes sarcastic attitude she was known for, but she couldn't see the humor. Every scene reminded her of something nice Colin did or said or an experience that drew them closer.

"Congratulations on a great video collaboration. I'm sure it will save your brand," Stuart said, bringing the video conference to a close.

After they signed off, Noelle turned to Gretchen. "Want to get a coffee?"

They grabbed their coats and headed to their favorite coffee shop down the street. It wasn't as cozy as Evergreen

Creek's cafe, but it would do. They ordered coffee and took a seat at a corner booth.

Gretchen jumped right in before Noelle could say a word. "Look, I'm sorry for going over your head and making that video, but it did the trick, didn't it? It saved your job."

"Yeah. I'm not upset. I know you had my best interest at heart."

"And my own, too. If you get fired, what am I going to do? I love working with you, and I've learned so much."

Noelle had been too caught up in her own misery to think about the ramifications for Gretchen if she lost her job. "You're right."

"Then why aren't you stoked?"

Noelle lifted one shoulder. "I'm bummed about leaving things the way I did with Colin. I mean, yeah, he jumped to conclusions, but that was no reason to ghost me. He wouldn't even let me explain."

"I'm sorry. It's all my fault. But I was worried and trying to save your career."

"I know." Noelle tried to express what she was feeling. "I just miss him. I know that sounds crazy because we just met, and he's not my type at all, but I can't explain it. I miss his face. I miss his voice. I miss the way he made me feel."

"You two were good together. It may not have been good for the show, but it was great for you personally." Gretchen drummed her fingers on the desk. "You should go back to Evergreen Creek. Make him talk to you.

"I tried. He doesn't want anything to do with me."

Gretchen touched the computer screen and scrolled through some of the videos they hadn't aired yet. "That's too bad, considering how happy he looks whenever the two of you are on screen together."

"Stop there," Noelle said when they came to the video of Noelle and Colin making mistletoe ornaments. "I have an idea."

"Oh?"

Noelle smiled for the first time since she returned to the city. "Let me work on this a little. We'll post the night before Christmas Eve."

Gretchen grinned. "Whatever you have in mind, I'll be there with bells on."

Noelle lifted her hand in the air, and Gretchen hit it in a high five.

Noelle outlined her plan. At first, Gretchen wasn't sure it would work.

"But it couldn't hurt, right?" Noelle asked.

They spent the next few hours going from store to store, picking up all the Christmas decorations they could find. Most of the shelves were picked over, but they bought enough to decorate Noelle's small apartment. They even found a tabletop tree in the clearance section.

"That should do it," Noelle said as they loaded their packages into the trunk of an Uber.

"Not yet," Gretchen said. "You need to buy something festive to wear. Something red and green and sparkly."

"I do?"

"Absolutely. What's a Christmas video if you don't dress the part?"

Noelle gave a deep sigh. "I think I may have reached the limit of my Christmas spirit."

When they reached Noelle's apartment, Gretchen told her to go inside and start decorating. She'd handle the rest.

Noelle wasn't sure whether to be relieved or a little frightened. She only hoped reindeer antlers weren't part of the Christmas outfit.

As it turned out, she was pleasantly surprised.

Gretchen returned with a tasteful silver sequined blouse Noelle could wear over a pair of black pants. She held up two necklaces — one with blinking Christmas lights, the other a simple strand of red and gold beads. "I'll take that one," she said, indicating the second one.

"Oh, thank goodness." Gretchen draped the blinking Christmas lights around her neck. "I wanted this one anyway."

It suited her.

Gretchen walked around the apartment, inspecting all the decorations they'd purchased. "You did a great job. It looks very festive."

"Best we could do on short notice, but yes, it's a step up from what I had before."

"Which was just a snow globe."

Noelle pointed to the shelf where the snow globe held a place of honor. "The tree is a little bare, but we can add more garland, and no one will notice."

"It'll make a nice backdrop." Gretchen gave an approving glance around the room. "Ready to start filming?"

"As soon as I change." Noelle crossed her fingers. "Wish me luck."

Gretchen gave her an encouraging smile. "If anyone can pull this off, it's you."

# Chapter Twenty-Five

Christmas Eve. It was the last day of the festival. Colin was exhausted but excited as well. Tonight, he'd cap off the closing ceremonies by playing Santa Claus and handing out gifts to the children. It was the highlight of the week, and he was a little bummed that Noelle wasn't there. Of all the days to film, this would be the one to cap off the series. Maybe it was just too holly-jolly for her. The cynic in her wouldn't find anything to bitch about, so she'd scurried out of town with her tail between her legs.

But he missed her.

He opened the door to the coffee shop, surprised when all heads spun around to stare at him. For a moment, he was afraid he had his shirt on backward or something. Then he realized they'd all been huddled around Max's laptop. Even Angela was there. She grabbed his arm and pulled him over to see what everyone was watching. It was Noelle's new video.

"She uploaded this last night," Max said. "We've already watched it twice."

Colin was prepared to see more videos of Noelle

trashing the town, but instead, she exuded sincerity. She wore a silver sequined blouse that reflected the Christmas lights around her.

"I came to Evergreen Creek expecting to feel superior," she said. "But instead, I found the true meaning of Christmas. I learned many lessons. I learned about family values and lasting friendships. I learned what it means to be a community of neighbors who occasionally disagree but always come together to help one another. I learned about loyalty, honesty, and love."

She held up the sprig of mistletoe they'd worked on together. Her eyes glistened. "And I learned to open up and let someone see the real me beneath all this bluster and bravado."

"Bluster and bravado?" Colin shook his head in amazement. "Is that what they're calling it these days?"

"Shhh!" Angela said.

Colin raised an eyebrow. Had Angela just shushed him?

"And so," Noelle continued, "this Christmas, my fondest wish is that everyone finds who they're looking for under the mistletoe." She looked directly into the camera, and Colin felt like she was staring straight at him. "Even me."

As she signed off, he wondered if she was talking directly to him.

"That was a surprise," Max said. "I'd heard rumors she'd burned her career to the ground."

"So," Colin said, "she found a way to revive her career, that's all."

Angela gave him a look that stopped him in his tracks. "You don't think she was talking about me, do you?" he asked.

"Obviously," she said. Everyone around the computer nodded their heads in agreement.

Colin looked from one to the other. "What do you expect me to do?"

"Go after her. You can fix this."

Colin shook his head. "It's the last night of the festival. There's too much to do. Who's going to play Santa?"

Geoff raised his hand. "I will!"

"There you go," Angela said. "Everyone will pitch in. You're free to go." She gave him a long, hard stare. "Before it's too late."

Still, Colin hesitated. Would she even want to see him, or was the video all for show? Did he have a chance?

Angela put it all into perspective. "You know your mother believed that Christmas was for being with the ones you love above all."

That was all the encouragement he needed. "Show Geoff where the Santa suit is." He leaned over and kissed the top of Angela's head. "And Merry Christmas if I don't see you tomorrow."

# Chapter Twenty-Six

NOELLE LOOKED AROUND. The apartment didn't look half bad. She'd strung fairy lights and garland along the door frames. Even though the tree was small, it was covered in makeshift ornaments and tinsel. Christmas music played softly in the background, giving the small apartment a holiday feeling.

The doorbell rang, and she opened the door to Gretchen, holding a charcuterie tray. "Wow," Gretchen said. "The place looks great!"

"I found a few more things this morning. It wasn't easy doing it on short notice. All the Christmas decorations were picked over. But I grabbed whatever I could find."

"I see you got more ornaments for the tree."

Noelle glowed. "I think it looks adorable." It was a small tabletop tree, but that meant she didn't have to buy a lot of ornaments. "It's no Evergreen Creek Christmas."

"No, but it's pretty good for your first-ever Christmas party. Who's coming?"

"A few people from work. Stuart said he'd be here. My

neighbor Bertie. And…" Noelle took a deep breath. "I invited my parents. Colin's always talking about family values. Let's see how that goes."

Gretchen put the appetizer tray on the counter and gave Noelle a quick hug. "It'll be fine. The question is, do you think Colin will show up?"

"Depends. If he sees the video. If he forgives me. If he ever wants to see me again."

"That's a lot of ifs."

"I could probably come up with a few more." Noelle straightened the wine glasses for the umpteenth time.

"Your nerves are showing."

"There's a lot riding on this."

The doorbell rang, and they looked at each other. "Ready?" Gretchen asked.

Noelle took a deep breath. "Ready as I'll ever be."

Stuart was the first to arrive. He gave Noelle a hug. "Congratulations," he said. "Today's numbers are through the roof!" He glanced around. "Cute apartment. Where's the bar?"

Noelle pointed him to the makeshift bar. "Help yourself."

He passed Gretchen on the way to the kitchen. "I hope you're livestreaming this."

"I will once the party gets started," she said.

He leaned close. "Do you think that mayor guy will show up?"

Gretchen held up her hand. "Fingers crossed."

Noelle opened the door for her next guest and caught her breath. "Mom!" She reached out and hugged her mother. It had been a long time, and they still had issues they needed to address, but it felt good to hold her mother close. She smelled like Noelle always remembered, a blend of talcum powder and Chantilly. "It's good to see you," she said.

"I was surprised to get an invitation. I'd been waiting. Hoping." Her eyes glistened. "I've missed you."

"I've missed you too, Mom." And to her surprise, Noelle meant it. God, she was growing soft.

Her mother stepped aside, and Noelle reached out to hug her mother's partner. She'd met Melissa the last time she'd been in Portland. They were good together, and her mother was the happiest she'd ever been. "Good to see you, Melissa."

"You look wonderful," she said. "Your mother and I watch all your shows. She's so proud of you."

That was surprising.

Her mother turned. "Is that handsome mayor going to be here?"

"That's the million-dollar question."

"Well, I hope he comes. I think he's a keeper." She reached out and stroked Noelle's cheek. "I can tell he makes you happy."

Noelle felt tears sting her eyes. It was true. Colin made her happy. His optimism diffused her cynicism. They balanced each other out.

"That's a pretty dress," her mother said.

Noelle smiled. In a sea of red and green Christmas outfits, she'd chosen a dress of baby blue. Only one person would understand the meaning behind it.

Next to arrive was her father and his third wife. She was young, thin, and blonde. Exactly her father's type. She handed Noelle a bottle of wine wrapped with a red bow. "Merry Christmas," she said.

"Thank you." What was her name? Carrie, Candy, Chloe? Whatever.

Noelle let them inside, then peeked out the door

behind them. No sign of Colin. She sighed and stepped inside, closing the door behind her.

The party was in full swing. Stuart was playing bartender, and Noelle was surprised to see her mother and father actually getting along.

Gretchen had started livestreaming. "We're getting a lot of traffic," she told Noelle. "Most of the comments are people wondering if Colin will show up."

Every time the doorbell rang, the entire room would hold their breath and wait, then release it when it was another guest and not Colin. The party grew louder and more raucous as the drinks flowed. Trying hard not to show her disappointment as midnight drew near, Noelle stepped outside for a breath of fresh air.

She stepped under the glow of the streetlamp and heard a familiar voice. "Merry Christmas. Or should I say Joyeaux Noel?"

"Colin! There you are!" She ran into his arms.

"My flight was delayed. I got here as soon as I could. And I brought this." He held up the sprig of mistletoe they'd worked on together.

Her heart leaped. She lifted her chin and met his lips with her own. The kiss was slow and gentle, exactly as she'd imagined it would be. His arms came around her waist, and he pulled her close. The kiss deepened as their bodies melded together. She could feel his heart pounding against hers. All she wanted for Christmas was to make this feeling go on forever.

When he broke away, he smiled. "I like your blue dress."

She stroked his sleeve. "And I like your blue shirt."

"I've searched for blue," he said.

"My whole life through," she answered.

"And now that I've found you, I'm never letting you go."

"That's not part of the poem."

"I improvised."

And with that, he lifted her off her feet and spun her around until she was dizzy, then set her down again and kissed her long and hard, setting her world spinning.

When he set her back on her feet, they both spoke at once. Colin laughed. "You first."

"I'm sorry for everything. I tried to make it right, but I kept messing up. Old habits die hard."

His voice was tender. "You have nothing to apologize for. You came to do a job, and I got in your way at every step. It wasn't my place to tell you how to do your job. What do they say? *If it ain't broke, don't fix it.*"

Maybe it needed fixing, though. She didn't have to lose her edge completely, but she could choose when sarcasm would be acceptable — and not use it if it would hurt someone else.

Colin cleared his throat. "Gretchen told me she was the one who altered that video. I'm sorry I didn't believe you. I was just so angry. That town means so much to me, and it looked like you were throwing mud all over it."

"I know. Gretchen thought she was saving my job. That doesn't make it right, but if you come inside, you can tell her that yourself."

"Do we have to go inside right this moment?"

"Yes, because I'm freezing out here."

Colin made an exaggerated sound of exasperation. "Okay, then, one more kiss before we go?"

She nestled into his embrace. "Well, since you brought the mistletoe all this way…"

They lingered over a long, slow kiss that held a world of promise. When they broke apart, Noelle walked him to her apartment. "Oh, I've been meaning to ask. You're not allergic to cats, are you?"

"Nope, why do you ask?"

When Berta brought the cat over, Damian was so glad to see Noelle he hadn't left her side. "Oh, you'll see," she said, then crooked her arm in his and walked him to her door.

# Chapter Twenty-Seven

NOELLE STRAIGHTENED Colin's bow tie. It flashed with green and red LED lights. She rolled her eyes, but a smile lit up her face. "Can you believe it's been a year?"

He lifted her hand and kissed it. The diamond engagement ring on her finger sparkled. He gestured to the decorated carriage they'd ride to the town square. "I don't think you'd have done this a year ago."

"Oh, I'd have done it all right. But I would have told my subscribers how cheesy I thought it was."

"And now?"

"It's still cheesy. But I kinda love it."

"That's because you love me."

"And you're the King of Cheese."

He made a mock bow. "At your service, my queen."

Gretchen pulled them aside for a quick video for Noelle's private channel, which was more popular than ever.

"Merry Christmas from both of us," Noelle said into the camera. "And as promised, you'll be video guests at our wedding. Tune in an hour from now when we'll be live streaming the ceremony."

Colin turned to the camera, more comfortable now than he was a year ago. "Assuming the bride doesn't get cold feet."

"Why do you think I'm marrying you?" she quipped. "My feet are always cold. I'm counting on you to keep them warm."

He wagged his eyebrows for the camera in a deliberately suggestive way.

They'd decided on a Christmas wedding since the holiday was so important to them both. Everyone who mattered was already in town, including her parents, who'd both tried to make up for lost time over the previous year.

Angela interrupted. "Are you two going to get on that carriage, or will I have to ride it for you?"

"Okay, okay." Colin gave Noelle his arm and helped her onto the carriage.

She gazed into his eyes. "Are we really doing this?"

"God willing, and the creek don't rise," he replied. "Not likely since the creek is frozen over."

She smiled. "Cheesy, like I said." But her laughter was with him, not *at* him. She'd come to love his cheesy humor because it came with a strong sense of loyalty and responsibility. She wouldn't have expected it in a million years, but here she was, in love with a man who could have stepped right out of the pages of a romance novel.

"Who said it was bad luck to see the bride before the wedding?" she asked.

Colin frowned. "Probably some wedding Grinch."

"I guess there's a Grinch for every occasion."

He put his arm around her. "Are you warm enough?"

She snuggled under the red velvet robe trimmed with

white fur that Angela had given her as a bridal shower gift. "Let's do this."

"Are you sure you're ready?"

She counted items off on each of her fingers. "I have something old — this necklace from my mother. And something new — the robe from Angela." She pulled it around her shoulders, burying her face for a moment in the faux fur. "I still need something borrowed and something blue."

"Something blue, huh?"

They shared a secret smile, remembering the poem they now had framed on the living room wall of the cabin they'd share once they were married. It was the same cabin he'd taken her to when their snowmobile had broken down. They'd already decorated the tree, complete with the silver ice skating ornament he'd given her last year. She couldn't wait to start their life together there.

Colin reached into his pocket and pulled out a single key on a keychain. He held it out to her.

"Cookie Monster? Let me guess. A Christmas gift from Angela?"

"You're getting good at this game."

She tucked the keychain into her bra.

"I'm going to need that back, you know. It's my snowmobile key."

"Of course. Now I have something borrowed *and* something blue."

He raised an eyebrow and glanced at her cleavage. "Remind me to retrieve that later."

Noelle smiled. "Oh, I will."

The carriage arrived at the town square. They'd lit the Christmas tree the night before, a Christmas Eve tradition in Evergreen Creek. An archway covered in evergreen and mistletoe stood in front of the tree.

Colin helped Noelle out of the carriage, then leaned over and kissed her forehead. "I'll see you at the altar in a few minutes."

She grinned. "If I don't run away."

His face grew serious. "Wherever you go, I'll find you."

"I'm counting on it." She gave him a little shove. "Now go stand where you're supposed to so your bride can make an entrance."

"My bride. I like the sound of that." The smoldering look on his face melted her to the core.

Noelle went into the clubhouse to prepare for the ceremony, where she was greeted by Gretchen and her parents, who'd requested the privilege of walking her down the aisle.

Gretchen, dressed in deep holly green, helped Noelle off with her robe. Her mother gasped, "Oh, you look so beautiful," she said with tears shimmering in her eyes.

Noelle turned to the mirror, admiring the lines of her white lace wedding gown. Gretchen helped her pin the veil in place, completing the image of a traditional bride. "Thank you for being my maid of honor," she said.

Gretchen shook her head. "I'm proud and honored that you asked me."

Noelle smiled. "Now, don't get all mushy on me. If you're going to cry, save it for the camera."

Gretchen laughed. "Same old Noelle."

But of course, that wasn't true. She wasn't the same person she was a year ago. She was softer, more secure. She no longer feared that those she loved would leave her. Colin had proved that to her and continued to prove it each and every day.

Gretchen handed her the bridal bouquet made of holly and mistletoe. "Ready?"

She took a deep breath. "Ready as I'll ever be."

"Okay." Gretchen grabbed her camera. "Give me five minutes to get down the aisle and set up the camera, then we'll be ready to roll."

Noelle waited five minutes, the longest five minutes of her life. Then, with her mother and father on either side of her and the wedding march playing in the background, she walked down the aisle to meet the man she'd be spending every day with for the rest of her life ... laughing all the way.

**The End**

**Linda Bleser** began her writing career publishing short fiction for women's magazines. Since then, she's published several award-winning novels in multiple genres, from rib-tickling comedy to bone-chilling suspense. Reviewers have hailed her work as unique, original, and impossible to put down.

Writing as both Linda Bleser and L.B. Milano, she has over a dozen books, short stories, and novellas in print. Linda is the proud recipient of the EPPIE Award, the Dream Realm Award, the Dorothy Parker Reviewers Choice Award, the Royal Palm Literary Award, and several readers' choice awards. She also received a top ten placement in the Preditors and Editors poll.

A transplanted New Yorker, Linda, and her husband have retired to sunny Florida, where she continues to dream up new stories on the beach.

**Mia Summers** is a sucker for love. There's nothing she likes better than snuggling up in a soft fleecy blanket with a hot cup of cocoa and an even sweeter romance to read the night away. Especially if she's reading about Hollywood heartthrobs or hunky hockey players. But after telling her best friend one too many times how she would have written the most recent novel, her friend blurted out, "Well then, why don't you write your own romance novels?" And that is exactly what Mia did.